Than[...]

I Loved [...]

Sweet Creek Holler

just Rolls off O's Tongue

Anne

Ms. Frances Lee
1202 Blakely Way
The Dalles, OR 97058

Sweet Creek Holler

Sweet Creek

HOLLER

Ruth White

Farrar, Straus & Giroux

New York

TO MY SISTERS
Audrey Virginia, Yvonne Marie,
and Eleanor June

For I do not want anyone to read my story carelessly.
I have suffered too much grief in setting down
these memories.

ANTOINE DE SAINT-EXUPÉRY, *The Little Prince*

Part One

1

When I—Virginia Carol Shortt—was just six my daddy was killed. My sister, June Marie, who was nine, read me all about it in the newspaper. It said my daddy, Jed Shortt, a coal miner for the Clancy Valley Coal Company, was shot in the back and the bullet came out under his arm. It said the man who shot him, Donald Struthers, was arrested and charged with "man's laughter." That's how Junie read it— man's *laf*-ter. When I asked Mama, who knew everything, what man's laughter was, she said, "It's not man's laughter, Gin-Gin, it's man-*slaw*-ter, and it means murder."

For a while there were so many neighbors and

kinfolks pouring in and out of our house, I didn't think much about murder and what it would mean to Mama and Junie and me. But then one day all the relations were gone, and the warm June sun threw a stillness over our little coal-company house. We moved around from room to room just touching stuff and looking at each other and wondering what was going to happen to us now that Daddy was gone.

Mr. Josh Clancy, the owner of the Clancy Valley Coal Company, came to see Mama and told her she would have to move out of the coal-company house. The houses in the camp, he said, were reserved for coal miners and their families, and the coal company let you live there for free as long as you worked for them. Mama just hung her head and said she didn't know what in the world she was going to do. Then Mr. Clancy looked like he wished he was someplace else.

"There's no hurry, Mrs. Shortt," he said to her. "I'll see if I can help you find a place."

That was in 1948, and me and Mama and Junie and Daddy had lived in Clancy Valley Coal Camp for as long as I could remember. It was a part of the coal-mining area nestled in the rugged Appalachian Mountains of Virginia's far western point.

All the houses were alike, square brown wooden boxes. There was a partition running down the middle of each house that separated the quarters of the two families living there. You went to the company store for food and clothes, and you paid with little tickets the company gave you. You went to the company doctor when you were sick, and he gave you medicine for free.

There was a movie house, too, in Clancy Valley that cost just ten cents to get in, and Daddy and Mama took us to lots of shows. And we got popcorn and ice cream. Now, if we had to leave and live in a new place, I wouldn't know what to act like. I'd never even seen another place except Coaltown, the county seat.

A few days later Mr. Clancy came back and said there was a house on Sweet Creek Holler three miles down the river that Mama could buy for only two thousand dollars. It was right below his own house, and he took Mama to see it.

That night Poppy came to visit us. Poppy was Daddy's daddy. He was an electrician in Mr. Clancy's mines. Me and Junie loved Poppy and Granny better than anybody else except for Mama and Daddy. Poppy was always laughing and joking and swinging us over his head like rag dolls, but that night he didn't laugh a bit. He sat with Mama in the kitchen and cried, and they talked real serious. I wondered where Granny was, but I didn't ask. There didn't seem to be a good time to butt in.

Finally, Poppy said he could raise a thousand dollars

for us. The other thousand Mama would get from Daddy's life insurance. So it seemed like we would be moving to Sweet Creek Holler.

Poppy borrowed a truck to move us and the way was long and hot because I had to sit all scrunched up amongst Mama and Junie and Poppy in the cab of the truck. I thought I would suffocate to death.

Sweet Creek branched off from the Levisa River valley over a big steel bridge. Then the truck started snaking up the dirt road to the house we were moving to. The holler was skinny between the mountains. The road was chiseled out of the side of one mountain base, and was just barely wide enough for the truck to travel without slipping into the creek. Houses were stuck on the sides of the hills, many with stilts underneath to prop them up level. Others had foot-bridges running from the road across the creek and on to the front porches. Some were made of cinder blocks, a few were white board, or brick, but most of them were tar-paper shacks.

People came out of their houses and stood on their front porches or in their little bitty yards to see who was passing by in a big truck all loaded down with stuff. Potbellied mamas carried their babies on their hips and squinted their eyes into the cab of the truck. Dirty young 'uns swung on a gate or twined their half-naked bodies around a porch post and looked at us. The men were still in the mines. Around every curve, a bunch of children scattered like chickens to get out of the road where they were playing marvels or jump rope, hopscotch or May I?, and twice Poppy had to slow the truck while first a pig, then a cow grumbled and moved out of the way.

I was getting pretty tired when all of a sudden we stopped beside a brown tar-paper shack and Poppy said, "This is it."

It was a four-room shack with a patch of weeds out front that was supposed to be the yard, and running alongside the road was an overgrown garden shaped like a piece of pie and ending at a bridge below. The house, yard, and garden were all closed in by a rusty wire fence with a sagging gate opening to the creek in back and another opening to the front. Across the creek, the mountains loomed straight up to the sky, and on the other side of the road in front, they humped up again. The mountains were all green in June, hunkering over the valley like bent-over giants, holding Sweet Creek Holler close in one deep wrinkle away from the rest of the world. The sky was a channel of blue you had to look straight up to see.

Poppy started unloading the truck, with Mama doing all she could, and they told me and Junie to stay out of the way. Then some men came by and offered to help. These were big rough men with coal dust all over them, on their way home from work.

They had hollow eyes and sharp features and hands like shovels. Poppy had told us that the men of Sweet Creek were independent miners who owned their own homes and were paid with money instead of company tickets.

Junie and I were standing beside the gate, watching and listening, when this little redheaded gal with her thumb in her mouth came up and gouged me. She held out a paper poke without saying a word. I took the poke and she turned around and ran back into the shack next door to ours. The poke wiggled. I peeped in, and out jumped this li'l ole puppy dog, just licking me all over and wagging his tail. He was a short, stumpy, brown armful. Me and Junie started giggling.

"Kain't we keep 'im, Mama? Huh? Please, Mama?" I begged.

"I reckon so, Ginny." She smiled at me and the puppy as she carried Daddy's RCA Victor into the house.

It didn't take long for the men to have everything in place in the house. Mama started fixing supper while Poppy thanked them for helping. Then Poppy got in the truck and hollered goodbye as he was driving off.

Supper was soup beans, fried taters, side meat, corn bread, and green onions. Mama thinned canned evaporated milk to wash down the corn bread. It was good.

After supper, me and Junie played with the puppy while Mama put things away. We bounced an old sock in front of his nose and watched him make for it. I found out if I let out a *Boo* sound with my lips right loud, that puppy would light into me like he was bound to tear me up. We got to giggling over that teeny dog thinking he was so big.

"You're funny and you're my buddy," I said to him.

"Buddy!" Junie said. "Let's call him Buddy."

"Okay," I agreed. "It's a good name."

The living room was bare, with a plain wooden floor. Our old familiar furniture—a blue messed-up couch, two matching chairs, a bookcase, a lamp table without a lamp to go on it, and a cedar chest with all of Daddy's stuff in it—somehow seemed out of place. I felt an emptiness and a longing for the old coal-camp house, and for Daddy, too.

Mama took some yellow crocheted daisies and tied back the dotted-Swiss curtains left behind by the last owners. Then she sat down to rest, and I climbed up on her lap.

"Will we ever see him again, Mama?"

"You mean Daddy?"

"Yeah."

"Who knows anything for sure, Gin-Gin."

"We'll see him in heaven, won't we?"

"That depends on what you make heaven out to be. As for me, I just don't know what heaven is."

"Mama, it seems to me heaven orta be a place where you see people you loved and who died."

"Maybe it is."

"Are we gonna starve, Mama?"

" 'Course not!"

"But can you feed me and Junie and you and Buddy, too?"

"I'll do my best."

"Will you have to get a job?"

"I might if I can. But what can a woman do? Schoolteaching's about all, and that takes a year of college. I just went to the eighth grade."

"But you can read real good."

Mama laughed a little. "That's because I was raised on the top of Grant Mountain, and there was nothing to do but read. So I got plenty of practice. It's a wonder I didn't go cross-eyed like my brothers said I would."

Mama sighed deeply and hugged me close. "We've got your daddy's Social Security. It'll have to be enough for now."

"Mama, was Daddy stealing something when he was shot?"

"What! Who in the world told you that?"

"I heard them men out there talking when they were helping us move in. They said Daddy was stealing something from Donald Struthers, and that's why he shot 'im."

"Well, that is a great big lie, Ginny Carol Shortt. Don't you ever believe such a thing about your daddy. He never stole a thing in his life."

"I was just saying what they were saying."

"Don't repeat things like that. That's how little stories turn into big, ugly lies. People are always talking about things they don't know nothing about."

Although Junie didn't like to sleep with me because I sometimes wet the sheets, we had always shared a bed until Daddy died. Then I naturally moved into bed with Mama. Now, in this new house, Junie could have slept by herself in her own bedroom. But she was afraid. She was too proud to say she was afraid, so I didn't say anything either. Her bed was moved in beside ours, and nobody ever said why.

That night I slept tight beside Mama in the dark June night to the sounds of catydids, crickets, frogs, and Sweet Creek rippling over the rocks in the dark outside our bedroom window. It was the first time I had the dream. I dreamed of a rosy room with a real high ceiling and a big, fancy, tinkling light with sparklers in it. It was a sitting room with a soft, rose-colored couch and all kinds of knicky-knacks scattered around on glass-topped tables. There was a funny noise all around me, in my head, filling me up. Like a clock maybe . . . no, lots of clocks. Yes, it was many, many clocks ticking together . . . tick . . . tock . . . tick . . . tock . . . real loud.

I came awake to the stillness, feeling like I lost something.

2

Next door to us were the Ratliffs, with nine children, from three months old to sixteen years, all boys except for two girls. In the morning the two girls stood at our front door and knocked.

"Hidy," I said.

"Hidy," the biggest girl said.

The other girl was the one who had handed me the puppy in the paper poke. Both had on feed-sack dresses, faded but clean. Both were barefoot and had washed-out blue eyes, a face so full of freckles you couldn't stick a pin between them, and coarse reddish-blond hair that curled up natural. You couldn't tell one from the other except for their sizes. Junie came up beside me and said, "I'm Junie and I'm nine."

"I'm Christine Ann and I'm eleven."

"I'm Ginny and I'm six."

The little Ratliff girl didn't say a word, and Christine Ann punched her. She stuck her thumb in her mouth.

"Well, she's Hilda Matilda," Christine said. "Folks call her Tildy. She's six, too."

Silence from Hilda Matilda.

Then we all struck off up the road together. Junie and I tried to talk about Roy Rogers and Dale Evans, but Christine and Tildy had never seen a movie, and they looked at us funny. I was beginning to think they didn't know anything, until we came up on the Clancy house.

It was the biggest house in Sweet Creek Holler. It had two floors, and it grew taller as we drew closer. It made the little shack on the hill across from it look like a chicken coop. There was a big yard, spread out like a green cloud all around, and these darker-green bushes trimmed up to look like big boxes all about the edges. The house sat farther back from the road than the other houses in the holler, on a kind of hump at a wide place in the valley where another thinner holler came into Sweet Creek.

"Clancys'," Christine said knowingly, tossing her head toward the castle.

"Oh, the man who owns the Clancy Valley Coal Company," Junie said. "Yeah. We know him. He found our house for us."

"They're strange folks," Christine said.

"Strange? How?"

"The old lady's a witch."

There was a mulberry tree shading the whole road and we sat down underneath, looking at the house.

"How'd you know she's a witch?" Junie said.

"We just know, that's all. For one thing, they keep horses. Nobody else in the holler got horses. They keep 'em up there in that old gray barn above the house."

"They've got horses," little Tildy piped in for the first time, proving she could talk. Then she popped her thumb back in her mouth. We gave her our full attention, hoping for more, but she'd had her say.

"They're real old horses," Christine went on. "Old and gray."

"Do they go out riding on 'em?" Junie asked.

"Never saw 'em. But listen . . ."

Then Christine told us a story.

It seemed the Clancys came down from Pennsylvania way back when because they inherited some mines in these parts. They bought up more mines, got rich as the Rockefellers, and decided to stay. Back then, there was old Mr. Tom Clancy, his wife the present witch, their son, Josh, and two little girls, Shirley and Lenora. They owned everything in sight, even the hills behind their house where there were mining roads crawling all over the place which ended in big black pits. These were abandoned mines.

Back there in that holler behind the house there

was also a stinking slate dump, Christine Ann told us, that burned all the time and smelled like rotten eggs. It was the dumping place for the mine waste. The coal trucks hauled the slate around the hills to a cliff and dumped it over the edge, where it slid for fifty yards or more and came to rest in the holler and on the side of the hill. By spontaneous combustion it produced little pockets of flame and made an ugly stink and an ugly sore against the bright hills. About the only time anybody ever saw Josh Clancy out on foot, she said, was in the fall time when he would check the fire to make sure it didn't spread to the dry leaves. And nobody hardly ever saw Mrs. Clancy, his mother, anymore. What happened was that ten years ago, in 1938, Mrs. Clancy and Josh went up to Pennsylvania to visit their kinfolks, and while they were gone, her old man went crazy as a mad dog and shot them two little girls, then his own self.

"You're making that up," Junie said.

"No, I'm not!"

"Shot 'em both dead?" Junie said in horror.

"Dead as a doornail."

"Then shot his own self?" I said.

"Blowed his own head off."

Me and Junie looked at each other with wide eyes. And Josh had seemed like an ordinary person.

"So the old lady buried them all," Christine went on. "And she's been holed up in that house ever since. Wouldn't come out if you set fire under her tail. Josh never took no wife. He takes care of his mother and all the mining business now."

"Who lives up there on the hill?" I pointed to the shack across the road from the Clancys'.

"Purvises live there. They got one girl, Lou Jean. She's eleven and perty as a pitcher. Here comes her daddy now, coming down the hill. He's a card."

Sure enough, a man was staggering down the hill from the shack, singing at the top of his lungs.

> *I come home this morning*
> *Drunk as I could be,*
> *And I saw a head laying on the bed*
> *Where my head orta be.*
> *"Wifey, little wifey,*
> *Come 'splain this thang to me:*
> *How come there's a head laying on the bed*
> *Where my head orta be?"*
>
> *"Ye blind fool, ye crazy fool,*
> *Kain't you never see,*
> *It's nothing but a cabbage head*
> *Yer granny sent to me!"*

The crazy song stopped and the man stopped and looked down at us sitting there in the middle of the road.

"Hallo!" he bellered.

"Hidy, Nit," Christine said.

"One . . . two . . . three . . . four . . ." he counted heads. "Four perty heads . . . perty, perty heads. And blow me down, two of 'em's strangers. Pertiest strangers I ever seed. And lookee here . . ."

Nit Purvis fumbled around in his pockets a bit, then brought out peppermint balls wrapped in clear paper.

"Betcha if I knowed these strangers' names I'd give 'em some candy."

We said our names quick.

Nit grinned and tossed four pieces of candy amongst us.

"Well, June Bug, Ginny Wienie, how old are ye? Forty? Are ye married, or old maids?"

We busted out laughing so hard I thought for sure I was going to pee on myself.

"Well, I betcha live in that house next to the Ratliffs, don'tcha?"

"Yep."

"And I betcha gotta grandpappy named Taylor Shortt, ain'tcha?"

"You know Poppy!"

"Do I know Poppy? Do a pig squeal? Do I know Poppy? He's my boss man, best boss man in the forty-eight states, and the best electrician in the whole wide world. Smartest man I ever seed!"

We grinned, proud.

"I'm Nit Purvis—call me Nit. Ask Poppy next time you see him don't he know Nit Purvis? Real name's Ezekiel, but folks call me Nit—short for Nitwit. That's what I am when I'm drunk, a nitwit. I do take a snort now and then. But I'm gonna quit one of these days. Makes my breath stink!"

Then Nit giggled like he had told a big joke. He was somewhere between thirty and sixty years old, tall and blond, wearing overalls and a T-shirt like all the men we knew.

"Where ya going to, Nit?" Christine said.

"To work, young 'un, going to work."

"Why, it's nearly ten o'clock," Christine went on. "Poppy Shortt'll fire your tail!"

"Fire me? No, he won't. He ain't expecting me till noon."

Nit grinned real big, showing beautiful white teeth; then he staggered on down the road, finishing his song.

> *I've traveled this wide world over*
> *A thousand times or more*
> *And a mustache on a cabbage head*
> *I never did see before!*

"Yeah, that Nit's a card," Christine said.

"I like him," I said.

"Everybody likes him, but he's got a mean woman

who'd drive the devil his own self to drink. And maybe if he didn't have his bottle he'd go crazy."

"What's the girl like?" Junie said.

"Lou Jean?" Christine smiled. "Everybody loves Lou Jean. She's perty and quiet and sweet."

"Let's go play," Junie said.

"Okay," Christine said. "Let's jump rope on Copperhead Bridge."

"What's a Copperhead Bridge?" I asked.

"That bridge yonder at the peak of y'all's property. It's told when that bridge was built they found a nest of copperheads there in the bank big as a heatin' stove."

"Snakes?" Junie said, shivering.

"But we ain't never saw even one," Christine went on. "It's a good place to jump rope."

Christine fetched her jump rope and we headed for Copperhead Bridge.

> *Mother, mother, I feel sick,*
> *Send for the doctor, quick, quick, quick!*
> *Doctor, doctor, shall I die?*
> *Yes, my child, but do not cry.*
> *How many horses will it take*
> *To carry me to the graveyard gate?*
> *One, two, three . . .*

Then you jumped until you missed, and that's how many horses you would need to carry you to the

graveyard gate. Never mind nobody had horses anymore, except the Clancys.

Directly, Mama let Buddy out of the house and he
came scampering and nipping around our feet, so
we couldn't keep the rope going. When we got the
silly giggles, we started making the *Boo* sound Buddy
hated so much. He started chasing us up and down
the road like he was going to eat off a foot if he
could!

And that was our first day on Sweet Creek Holler.

3

The next evening after supper we got a handwritten
invitation to a candy party at the Purvises'. Christine
delivered it.

> WHAT: A candy party
> WHERE: At the Purvises
> WHEN: When you get here
> SIGNED: Lou Jean Purvis

It was our first candy party, and we dressed up in
our best dresses. Mine was white with blue bears
embroidered on the pockets, and Junie's was green.

We wore our white patent-leather shoes Daddy had bought us for Easter, and Mama plaited our fine yella hair in pigtails. Then she made us wash our ears and necks real good. Mama was shy and didn't want to meet a lot of strangers at a party. "I'll go next time," she promised us.

But we knew Mama would never go to a party.

"Ask Mrs. Ratliff if you can walk home with her," Mama said as we were leaving. "I'll wait up for you."

The Purvis house, though small and cramped, was clean as a dinner plate. It looked like Mrs. Purvis must have scrubbed the floorboards and washed the white curtains which were blowing at the open windows. There were even little sprigs of wild flowers stuck around on the dressers and places like that.

In spite of what Christine had told us about Mrs. Purvis being so mean, she managed to grin at everybody that night. She wore a fresh-smelling dress that used to be blue, and her frizzy gray hair was caged in a fine net.

And there was Lou Jean, as pretty and sweet as Christine said she was. Dolled up in a little red sundress with white sandals, she looked for all the world like Shirley Temple.

"I wanted to have a party so I could get to know y'all," she chirped, and squeezed mine and Junie's hands. "Mama didn't want to let me, but Pa helped me beg her. Come, let me show you something."

She took us into a small, cluttered kitchen, and there spread out on the table was enough candy to stock a store.

"Miz Moore sent the nutty fudge." Lou Jean grinned, showing dimples in her pink cheeks. "And Miz Jenkins sent the seafoam. Miz Looney made the caramel . . . I could just bust . . ." Lou Jean giggled like she was tickled to death. "And Mama made a lot of Kool-Aid."

"We didn't bring a thing," Junie said, embarrassed.

"Oh, my goodness! That don't matter," Lou Jean said. "You and Ginny . . . why y'all are the guests of honor! When you're the guests of honor, you don't have to bring a thing!"

"Guests of honor?" Me and Junie exchanged glances. "Us?"

"Come on and let me tell everybody else," Lou Jean said, and led us back into the living room, her face flushed with excitement.

"Lookee here, everybody!" she announced. "This here's Ginny and Junie Shortt. They're the guests of honor. Let's make them feel welcome."

"Hidy do, Ginny, Junie," the children said, and they clapped for us till I felt like I was on the Grand Ole Opry. That's how Lou Jean was, I learned that first night, always trying to make other people feel good. Then she put me and Junie in the two best chairs in the room and pulled a straight-back chair between us for herself.

"First we're gonna play 'My Ship's Coming In.' Junie, you start off."

It was a good party. We played all the same games we had played in Clancy Valley whenever we got together with two or more children for any occasion. It seemed everybody everywhere knew the same games we did. After "My Ship's Coming In" we played Spin the Bottle, Drop the Clothespin, Button Button, In This Circle, and Whatcha Got There?

> *Whatcha got there?*
> *A bag of nits—*
> *Well, shake it till it spits!*

Then the first one to move would get shook until his teeth clacked together.

When we were tired of games, Mrs. Purvis brought out the candy. We ate until we felt sick. Then the grownups starting drifting in. They acted like they came to pick up their young 'uns, but directly they started eating candy and drinking Kool-Aid, then telling stories and jokes. Dewey Jenkins and Jess Ratliff were funny enough, but Nit Purvis made us laugh till we cried.

"You know how hot it's been lately?" he said. "Well, it's been so hot the pigs all melted up there in my pen, and the grease rolled down in my tater patch. Now we got a hillside full of French fries!"

The singing started up.

> *Where did you get that dress, little girl?*
> *And the shoes that are so fine?*
> *I got my dress from a railroad man*
> *And my shoes from a man in the mine.*

Lou Jean's voice rose pure and sweet above the others, while Christine did a fine alto. Afterwards Nit and Jess sang my favorite while Dewey played the guitar, and us little ones did the echo.

> *Down in the valley,*
> *Valley so low,*
> *Late in the evening,*
> *Hear the wind blow.*

Then Lou Jean did a solo left over from the war years, and just about every woman in the room cried before she was finished.

> *They say one winter day*
> *He left his loved one,*
> *With a vow he'd return*
> *When the fields were green with spring.*
> *Though springtime came, it didn't bring*
> *Her loved one.*
> *Now at night from her door*
> *You can clearly hear her sing,*

"Open door, open arms
Wait for your safe return.
Day and night there's a light
In my heart that will burn.
Let the light lead you home
Through the wide open door
Straight into my open arms
Forevermore!"

The room fell quiet. I guess the older ones were thinking of the kinfolks they lost during the war. Will Jenkins, who was thirteen, and who I later heard had lost a brother in the Phillipines, looked at Lou Jean with big soulful eyes, and I noticed she blew him a sweet little kiss. I put my head on Lou Jean's shoulder, wanting some of her attention and feeling lonesome even in a room full of people. She put one arm around me and whispered, "You're so sweet, Ginny. I want you and Junie to be my best friends."

Best friends with this creature the fairies brought! It seemed almost more than I could take in.

Mamas started whispering their good nights to Mrs. Purvis, and wrapping up their sleeping babies. Bunches of people grouped together to walk up or down the holler to their houses. The men went ahead, and the women and children followed. I stumbled along, half asleep, holding Junie's hand. Mrs. Ratliff, Christine, Hilda Matilda, and the Ratliff boys walked close by. Others came behind. One was Mrs. Moore and her herd of young 'uns. Seemed like she had about twenty. We were passing the dark Clancy house when Junie all of a sudden jerked my hand real hard.

"What'sa matter?" I said.

"Lookee there," she whispered, motioning toward the Clancys' front porch.

I looked, but didn't see anything. "What is it, Junie?" I said.

Junie started to say something else, but a loud whisper interrupted her.

"She's out to steal somebody's man!" the voice said.

"Who?" somebody else said.

"The Widder Shortt!" came the first voice again.

Junie had paused in the middle of the road to look back over her shoulder at the Clancy house, but the sound of Mama's name brought her around, and we exchanged glances.

Mrs. Ratliff bent over the two of us, and whispered, "That's Nellie Moore running her mouth. She don't know y'all are here with me. Now, don't let her git to you. Her tongue ain't hinged to her brain. It runs all by itself."

I looked at the blob in the dark which was Mrs. Moore.

"She puts on lipstick to go to the store," the blob went on. "Now, tell me what she does that for if she ain't after somebody's man?"

"She ain't seen one worth stealing yet," Christine

hollered as she put her arm around me. "But in case she gets desperate, Miz Moore, you best keep that old bald-headed thang of yours locked up!"

The group busted out laughing and I grinned in the dark. Guess that would shut Mrs. Moore up for a while, and sure enough it did.

Mama was waiting up for us as she had promised. We didn't say a word to her about Mrs. Moore's big mouth, because it would hurt her feelings. And we were too tired to tell her much about the party, so we washed our sticky hands and faces and tumbled into bed. Mama stayed in the kitchen and washed her own self a bit.

"Ginny," Junie whispered across the room to me.

"What?"

"Ginny, didja see 'em?"

"See what?"

"At the Clancy house when we passed by it. Didn't you see?"

"I didn't see nothing, why?"

"On the porch, Ginny. You swear you didn't see nothing?"

"I swear."

"Will you swear, too, that you won't tell nobody in the world?"

"Tell nobody what?"

"Just swear!"

"I swear."

"There were two little girls standing on the Clancy porch in the dark, just staring at us when we passed by."

4

For the rest of that golden summer Lou Jean, Christine, and Tildy came out to play with me and Junie almost every day. They showed us their favorite places in Sweet Creek Holler, the best cliffs and caves, the hidden mountain streams and cool grassy spots where a playhouse could be made.

We found knobby green apples so bitter they stung our taste buds. We discovered sour grass and mud dobbers, and once Buddy treed a possum, which tickled us no end.

Sometimes we happened on blackberry bushes loaded down, and picked gallons. Mama canned them in Mason jars and stacked them up on shelves in the extra bedroom.

"When winter comes," Mama said, "we'll open them and stew them; then we'll eat them with butter and biscuits, so that we can taste some of the summer sun even when it snows."

Me and Junie also found something special in being

sisters that summer. We made daisy chains for each other's hair, and maple-leaf skirts. One day we were plucking poke greens off the hillside by the road, and I said, "Nobody's said a word, Junie. Nobody else saw 'em."

"You never told nobody, didja?"

"No! I been listening and waiting to hear somebody else say they saw something. You know I wouldn't tell a secret."

"I know it, Ginny. You know, I love Lou Jean, but you're really my best friend. I can tell you things and you don't laugh at me."

I grinned. I could tell her things too, like my dream about the rose room, and she didn't laugh at me either.

"I'll finish the greens, Junie. You done filled up most of the bucket."

"But you're littler than me, Ginny. You can't do as much."

I worked faster.

"Ginny, I think it really was them I saw."

"The dead Clancy girls, you mean?"

"Yeah, it had to be them. And maybe the reason I was the only one who saw them was 'cause I was the only one who looked," Junie said.

"Could be," I agreed.

"Still," Junie went on like she was talking more to herself than to me, "they were plain as day, even in the dark. It was almost like they were lighted up or something."

We were hauling the bucket of greens between us going home when Lou Jean came trotting down the road all bubbly and laughing. She was wearing a neat little blue dress the same shade as her eyes, and her yella hair was flying in the breeze behind her.

"Mama's feeling poorly but she said I can go to the revival as long as y'all go with me," Lou Jean said breathlessly.

"The revival!" Junie and I said together.

"Yeah," Lou Jean continued. "Please say you'll go! Please! Please! Everybody'll be there. And we'll hear about Jesus the Lord Our Saviour."

Naturally me and Junie wanted to go, and when we said yes, Lou Jean started squealing and jumping up and down and hugging us both at once.

We had recently learned that the revival at the Church of Jesus Christ was second in importance only to the county fair. For the past week, preachers had driven their Chevrolets up and down the holler, visiting folks, always grinning and red-faced, inviting us all to come.

Now our mama and daddy never went to church or told us about Jesus, but they didn't care if we learned about him somewhere else. They simply didn't have it clear in their own heads what they believed, so they let us pick and choose what we wanted to. Lou Jean's mama was real big on Jesus. She had a picture of him on the cross right over their kitchen table.

The church bus picked us up in front of our house and carried us all the way to the mouth of the holler, where the church stood tucked into the side of the mountain. That first night, just about everybody and his cousin was there. They had to drag chairs into the aisles, and still some people were left standing. There were five evangelists, grinning and sweating. It sure was close in that tiny church.

The visiting speaker that night was Little Brother Arkansas, a sixteen-year-old powerhouse, full of the love of God, all dressed up in white right down to his shoes. He was real short for his age, and Lou Jean, sitting beside me, kept on giggling, whispering that he was about the cutest feller she had ever seen.

First, Little Brother told us how he had come to accept the Lord into his heart way up there in Arkansas when he was twelve years old. He had lived in the Ozarks, he said, and did all kinds of evil things, like smoking corn silks, and peeping into the cracks of the girls' outhouse at school. Then one day, when he was in the mountains, just taking in all the beauty of nature, the hand of the Lord took ahold of him, and he heard a voice tell him that from that day forward he was to give his heart to Jesus and preach His holy word wherever the Lord called him.

Lou Jean wasn't giggling anymore. She was listening to Little Brother with a look of heavenly rapture on her pretty face.

Little Brother's sermon was about hell and all its horrors. He said if you didn't give ten percent of everything you had to Jesus you would go there for sure. So when the plate was passed around you never saw so many quarters and even fifty-cent pieces. Then he started begging folks to come to the altar and confess their sins to the Lord. I liked that part best. Everybody cried, and all the lost sinners, including Lou Jean, started to go up to the front and fall on their knees before Little Brother Arkansas.

We were singing "Just As I Am" while Little Brother stood up there crying and pleading, "Come to Jesus, sinner." Blue-eyed and blond, in his spotless suit, I imagined he was the Christ Child his own self. I wanted to be saved with Lou Jean, but Junie held me back.

"Come on, Junie, let me go!" I pleaded. "I wanna confess my sins."

"You ain't got no sins, stupid," Junie whispered, embarrassed to death. "Now, hush up or I'll pinch you."

"I wanna go to Jesus!"

"*He* ain't Jesus! Be still!"

So I wasn't saved that night, but Lou Jean was. Little Brother had scared the devil out of her. On the way home, she sat between me and Junie on the bus as quiet as dawn, and she was trembling.

"You think it's true, Junie?" she whispered in the dark. Even her voice was trembling.

"What? What's wrong, Lou Jean?" Junie said.

"What he said about burning in hell. Is it true?"

"I don't know, Lou Jean," Junie said. "But you got nothing to worry about. You're saved."

"I might not be good enough. Is it in the Bible about hell?"

"I reckon."

"I hate fire, Junie. I burned my hand once, and it was the worst pain."

Lou Jean fell silent then, but we could still feel her trembling between us all the way home.

5

From as far back as I could remember, there were books in our house. Both Mama and Daddy were always reading something or other, sometimes to their own selves quiet, not moving their lips a bit;

sometimes aloud to each other, and laughing at things I didn't understand; sometimes aloud to me and Junie. Now, on these lazy summer evenings, me and Junie huddled around Mama on the old blue couch while she read to us from *The Secret Garden*. It was my first taste of a real novel, and I could see it was going to take many nights to finish it all. The evenings stretched out comfortable and sweet with the funny little English girl in the book. I felt like I knew her.

One evening in late August, Mama's voice was growing weary from reading when we heard the sound of a car coming up Sweet Creek Holler, and headlights swung over Copperhead Bridge. Mama stopped reading and we watched the lights burn a hole in the darkness. Then lo and behold the car stopped right in front of our own gate. Me and Junie tumbled over each other trying to get out on the porch.

It was Poppy in a Coaltown taxi.

"Poppy!"

He was laughing and whooping it up as he left the taxi and came inside, swinging us above his head, "bearding" our cheeks. He smelled like whiskey.

"Give poor ole Poppy a kiss!"

We kissed him and he dug candy bars out of his shirt pocket. Brocks and Baby Ruths.

Mama sat on the couch, smiling.

"You okay, Olivia?" he said to her.

"I'll do, Taylor. How's Sadie? She holding up all right?"

"She's all broke up, Olivia. I reckon time heals all wounds like they say, but right now she's all broke up."

I knew they were talking about Daddy dying, but I concentrated on the candy and tried not to think of Granny being all broke up.

"Where's your fiddle, Poppy?" I said.

"I didn't bring my fiddle, Ginny. But tell you what, me and Granny'll come on Labor Day and bring you a watermelon, and I'll bring my fiddle, too. How's that?"

"Fine."

Poppy settled himself on the blue chair, and I curled up in his lap. Oh, how I loved the smell of his hair and the tobacco in his shirt and the whiskey on his breath. He smelled just like Daddy.

"So you'll be starting school, Ginny Carol?" he asked.

"Reckon so," I said.

"Well, you better learn to read and write real good, and mind the teacher."

"I will."

The taxi horn blew.

"Told him I'd be here no more'n five minutes," Poppy said. "Now, Ginny, Junie, you girls be good and make Poppy proud of you."

"You brought a taxi all the way up here just for five minutes?" Junie asked.

"Naw, that's my friend, Barney Keene, driving that taxi. You know he won't charge me nothing."

"Glad you could stop by, Taylor," Mama said. "Come when you can stay longer, and bring Sadie, you hear?"

"I'll do it, Olivia. You need anything?"

"Lordy, I reckon we need about everything, but we ain't hurting for nothing."

"Well, you know you can call on me if you need anything. Send word by Nit Purvis."

"I will. I appreciate all you've done."

"Like your house, girls?"

"It's okay."

"Then give poor ole Poppy a kiss, and he'll be gone."

"You won't forget Labor Day?" I said.

"No siree. I won't forget."

After the kisses he left in the taxi. Me and Junie stood gazing out the window long after he was gone.

On Labor Day we woke up early, dressed in shorts, and parked on the front porch to wait for Poppy and Granny to come with the watermelon. Buddy darted around chasing his tail and jumping all over us for attention; then after a while Lou Jean came down the road. She was trying to teach me and Junie how to whistle. Junie was doing pretty good, but I had so many teeth missing I couldn't get any traction. It was aggravating.

"Let's play like," Junie said.

"Okay," I said. "Play like we're singers on the Grand Ole Opry."

"I'm a gospel singer!" Lou Jean said excitedly, clapping her hands together.

So we played like. Lou Jean was a real good singer, and it got so after a while we were believing she really was a gospel singer on the Grand Ole Opry and we were her audience. Our playing like was that real. Even Mama came to the door and listened.

"A car's coming!" Junie said directly.

It was a '46 Ford and we strained our eyes till it passed, but it wasn't Poppy.

"Let's play like we're going on a trip," Junie said. "Where we going?"

"Yeah, anywhere in the world we want to go," Lou Jean said.

"What about Pikeville, Kentucky?" I said. "I have always wanted to go there. Daddy went there once to a union meeting."

"Okay, we're going to Pikeville, Kentucky," Lou Jean and Junie agreed.

So the game went on through most of the afternoon, and still no Poppy and Granny.

We started playing with Buddy and got all dirty. Then Lou Jean had to go home.

"They ain't coming," Junie said as we trudged into the house.

"People shouldn't break promises," I said. "It's mean."

"He didn't mean to break a promise," Mama said. "He had something else to do, or he just forgot. Folks do forget sometimes."

"But he's always saying he's going to do something and he don't," Junie said. "Like he said he was going to buy us a refrigerator, remember? And I bet he never will."

"He will," Mama said. "He will when he gets the money."

"He's got the money!"

But we didn't see Poppy for a long time.

6

The first day of school I dressed up in my white dress with the blue bears on the pockets. Outside our gate, Christine, Tildy, Lou Jean, and the Ratliff boys were waiting for us. Junie and I joined them and we set off together, walking to the school a mile and a half down the road.

On the way Christine advised us newcomers on how to act, what to do and say to keep from being pure-tee fools.

"Don't never scratch your head," she said. " 'Cause the minute somebody sees you scratching, they get the word out you got lice, see? And onst the word gets out you got lice, you might as well shoot yourself and be done with it."

We took that in. Never scratch.

"And don't never cross your legs when a boy's leaning down to reach in his desk. 'Cause if you do, he'll say he seen something whuther he did or not."

It had been raining and the coal trucks had been hauling coal up from the head of the holler, making deep, black ruts of mud. Buddy came trotting along in the mud just like he was supposed to be going along.

"Get on home!" I hollered at him, but it didn't do a bit of good. That dog was bound he was going to school.

"Just let 'im be," Christine said. "He'll get tired waiting outside and he'll go home. Just hope Miz Mitchell don't see 'im."

"Who's Miz Mitchell?"

"She's the principal and the sixth-grade teacher."

"What'll she do if she sees him?"

"She'll whoop 'im."

"No, she won't!"

"She will if she's a mind to."

"Go home, Buddy!" I hollered. "Go home!"

But Buddy was going to school.

The mud got thicker as we went along. If you stayed on the edge of the creek where the weeds were, it was easier to walk, but then the bank fell away in places and you could go sliding right down into the water. Having shoes on for the first time in months was bad enough, but having them packed with mud was about more than I could stand. And having to worry about Buddy getting whooped by the principal was worse yet.

"I ain't going," I announced and stopped in my muddy tracks.

"You are too going," Junie said.

"No, I ain't."

"You have to go."

"What'll happen if I don't?"

"They'll put you in jail."

"They won't do it."

"They will too do it!" Christine said.

Then Lou Jean put her arm around me and said sweetly, "Come on, Ginny, honey, get on Bubba's back. He'll haul you . . . Bubba?" she said to the biggest Ratliff boy. "Won't you bend over and put this young 'un on your back? Her feet's so little she just can't handle all this mud."

Bubba's face turned a queer shade of purple. If anybody else but Lou Jean had asked him that, he would have laughed.

"I reckon," he mumbled. "But I ain't hauling her on the school ground."

"You don't have to. Just carry her out of this mud. You're such a nice boy, Bubba."

Then brother Clevis was drafted to carry little Tildy.

Riding on Bubba's back wasn't half bad, except I had to hold my feet straight out to keep from bumping mud on his clean overalls.

"Don't you tell nobody I packed you," he muttered. " 'Cause if you do, they'll call me a big old sissy, and I swear I'll have to stomp somebody's tail for it, and it might be yourn."

"I won't tell, Bubba."

"Another thing," Christine prepared to give us one last bit of advice. "Don't have nothing to do with them Weed children. They's pure trash."

The Weeds made up the "bad" element of Sweet Creek Holler. They were no poorer than all the other poor people of the holler, but they were on relief, and they were dirty. I asked Mama one time if we were on relief, and she said no, Social Security was respectable because it was earned. Not to earn your beans seemed to be the worst thing a person could do. Word was around that the Weeds ate fried lizards for breakfast and used a hole in their floor for a toilet. The girls in school were Daisy, Rose, and Tulip; the boys were Clover, Birch, and Goldenrod. I secretly admired the spunk of Mrs. Weed to give her children such names. Seems like she brooded on the condition of her life and a name like Weed, and not being able to do a thing about it, she decided to give her children something special.

Sweet Creek Elementary School was perched up on the hillside above John Looney's store where Cripple Creek ran into Sweet Creek. I had a nickel in my shoe so I could buy a bottle of pop at lunchtime from the store to eat with my baloney sandwich.

"Git down now," Bubba said when we got near school. "Walk on your own two legs."

I crawled off Bubba's back and we all started up the hill. There were children everywhere. Buddy trotted along beside me and through the crowd of children right up to Mrs. Brown's classroom.

"You stay right 'cheer until it's time to go in," Christine told me and Tildy.

Then the big girls disappeared into the crowd. There were four rooms at the school. Mrs. Brown had the first grade and half the second grade in one room; Mrs. Simpson had the other half of the second grade and all of the third grade in the second room; Mrs. Mason had the fourth grade and half the fifth grade in the third room; and Mrs. Mitchell had the other half of the fifth grade and all the sixth grade in the fourth room. Tildy and me would be in Mrs. Brown's first grade, Junie in Mrs. Mason's fourth grade, and Lou Jean and Christine in Mrs. Mitchell's sixth grade. After the sixth grade you had to go away to Coaltown to the high school.

Mrs. Mitchell rang a big cowbell and we all piled into our rooms. Mrs. Brown was a young, pretty woman with brown hair and gray eyes. She flashed a big smile with lots of teeth in it all over the place. Tildy settled down right in front of me and stuck her thumb in her mouth.

And here came Buddy. He lay down on the floor beside me. I acted like I didn't see him. Mrs. Brown started talking about *read-ing* and *writ-ing*. She didn't chop the "ing's" off the ends of her words like most folks. But that made sense after she told us she spent two whole years at Radford Teachers College. I decided she must be about the smartest person in Sweet Creek Holler.

All of sudden Mrs. Brown stopped talking and looked straight at Buddy. "What is that?" she hollered out, and pointed at him like she never did see a dog before in her life.

Nobody said a word, but everybody looked at me

and Buddy. I looked at my gnawed-off fingernails.

"What is that?" she said again.

"It's a dawg," this little curly-headed girl said.

"That is correct, Susie Ruth, it is a dog," Mrs. Brown conceded. "Can a dog learn to read? Can a dog learn to write?"

"No, ma'am," Susie Ruth said. "He kain't."

"Then why is this dog in school?"

Nobody could answer that one.

"Whose dog is he?" Mrs. Brown said and looked right at me. "Maybe the owner of this dog can tell us why her dog is in school?"

Still no answer.

"I will ask one more time. Who owns this dog?"

"Ginny," Tildy said her first word of the day, then promptly stuck her thumb back in her mouth.

"Ginny," Mrs. Brown said to me. "You are Ginny?"

"Yeah."

"Say, 'Yes, ma'am.'"

"Yes, ma'am."

"Does that dog belong to you, Ginny?"

"What dawg?"

"The dog at your feet, my dear."

"Oh!" I looked down at Buddy. "I declare! Where'd he come from?"

"Is he yours?"

"Yes, ma'am."

"Ginny, you must remove your dog from the classroom and never bring him to school again."

"I didn't bring him to start with."

"Just put him out."

Mortified, I got up and left the room. Buddy followed me. With so many sticky bodies crowded together, and it being September, the classroom door had to be left open.

Outside, I stomped my foot at Buddy. "Now, stay!"

Then I walked back in, and Buddy walked back in.

The children giggled.

I went out again. Buddy went out again. I stomped at him again. I said "Stay!" again. I went back in and Buddy went back in.

The same thing happened the third time, and the class was bustin' up.

Mrs. Brown's lips got tight.

"Put him out and close the door, Ginny," Mrs. Brown said.

Everybody groaned.

I did as I was told and Buddy began to whine at the door. Mrs. Brown's lips got tighter.

Clover Weed was spending his second year in the second grade after spending two years in the first grade, so he was a whole head taller than the other children in Mrs. Brown's room. It didn't take me long to see he had well earned his reputation as the meanest boy in Sweet Creek Holler. He started making a noise that sounded like a great big poot every time Mrs. Brown turned her back on him. All the second-grade boys laughed behind their hands, but the second-grade girls and all the first-graders just sat scared and stone-faced, because maybe the teacher might think it was them that did it.

Buddy went on scratching and whimpering, and I didn't know who was more aggravated, him or Mrs. Brown. She knew Clover Weed was making that poot sound, but she couldn't catch him. It was hard for her to go on talking about ABCs and 1, 2, 3s with Buddy carrying on and Clover Weed acting up.

Mrs. Brown wrote *boy, girl, cat, dog* on the chalkboard and talked. I listened and looked, expecting to learn to read at any moment, but the ABCs did not make words to me. C-A-T might as well have been "dog," and G-I-R-L might as well have been "boy," for all the sense they made to me.

"Now, how many of you nice girls and boys can print your name?"

All the second-graders proudly raised their hands, and some of the first-graders, including me, raised our hands too.

"Then you must print your name for me very large on a piece of paper and show it to the class. I will print for those who cannot do so; then you may copy what I print."

I printed

Ginny

on my paper, and waited, proud, for Mrs. Brown to come to my desk.

Clover Weed threw something across the room, and it landed on Tildy's head.

"*Eee-ow!*" Tildy let out a scream she must have saved up for six years. A dead green lizard fell off her head and onto her lap. Tildy jumped up, dumping the lizard on the floor, while the second-grade boys whooped it up. Tildy jammed her thumb into her mouth and silently jumped up and down. She looked so funny the rest of us had to laugh, too.

"Here! Here!" Mrs. Brown clapped her hands together. "What's the meaning of this?"

"Ooooo . . . Its guts are falling out!" little Susie Ruth cried when she saw the dead lizard on the floor. Then she clutched her belly and left the room. Buddy came trotting in. In all this racket, nobody noticed him but me.

"Who is responsible for this?" Mrs. Brown demanded.

Hearing Mrs. Brown's mad voice, Buddy slunk up an aisle on the second-grade side of the room, his tail between his legs. The room got quiet.

"I will not stand for this," Mrs. Brown said, her

face as red as a tomato. She didn't know what to do. She walked to the window and closed her eyes like she was praying.

"*Pooo-ooot!*" Clover Weed let out his nasty sound so loud you could hear it next door.

It happened that Buddy was slinking past Clover's desk at that moment, plenty scared already, and that noise just about made him jump out of his hide. He pounced on Clover Weed and lit into him with all his little puppy teeth, making enough noise for five grown-up dogs. It looked like he was bound to kill Clover Weed.

Clover started hollering, "Git 'im off'n me! Git 'im off'n me!"

But the rest of us were so startled we couldn't do a thing but stare, with all our eyes and mouths wide open.

"Ginny!" Mrs. Brown came alive. "Call off your dog."

"Buddy! Come 'ere, Buddy!" I screamed.

Right off, Buddy turned back into a li'l ole puppy dog and trotted to me, wagging his tail. Clover Weed was blubbering and crying like a baby. He had these bloody places all over his arms and rips all over his pants.

"Durn fool dawg!" he whined. "Durn dawg. Look what he done, Miz Brown."

I was scared. What if Mrs. Brown called in the

principal and they whooped Buddy? What if they hurt him bad? But Mrs. Brown did a funny thing then. With her face as calm as clouds, she went on with the name printing just like nothing ever happened. She left the door open and acted like Buddy wasn't even there.

At lunchtime I heard all the teachers laughing together in Mrs. Mitchell's sixth-grade room, and I plainly heard Mrs. Brown say, "Why, he's the best dog in Virginia!"

Whenever I looked up from my work the rest of the day, there was Mrs. Brown looking at Buddy where he lay jerking around in his sleep, dreaming about chasing possums. And playing around Mrs. Brown's mouth was this funny little smile.

Clover Weed seemed to fade into his desk. He didn't say anything more. And it was understood that a dog had joined the first grade.

As fall turned to winter, I started liking Mrs. Brown and she liked me. She brought scraps of food for Buddy to eat. Sometimes Clover would act up a little, and Mrs. Brown would say real sneaky-like, "That Buddy is the best dog in Virginia. I think he would do just about anything Ginny told him to do."

And Clover would shut up.

I liked the smell of chalk dust, so that ever after, whenever I smelled it, I remembered those quiet fall days in Mrs. Brown's room with Buddy at my feet, when letters turned into words for the first time and words turned into ideas. Reading became an obsession. I read the labels on mayonnaise jars and cornflake boxes. I wrote my name on every rock and tree. I spelled out all the names of people I knew. I read funny books, movie-star magazines, and the Bobbsey Twins, and Junie patiently told me the words I didn't know.

Then winter came on. Christmas was on the way.

7

Christmas Eve, Mama made cocoa and floated little lumps of butter on top of each cup. This was always our special Christmas treat. We had a stumpy pine tree with paper ornaments Junie made in school set up in the warm front room where the heatin' stove was. Ever so often, Mama added another shovelful of coal. Even though Poppy was sending loads of coal to us regular, we didn't like to waste much of it, but Mama said it was all right to use more coal than usual on Christmas Eve.

We slurped our cocoa and huddled around Mama while she read to us *Why the Chimes Rang*. She read it soft and easy, so you had to quit wiggling around and listen close.

After the story I asked Mama what time it was, for the fortieth time, and she said, "Eight or better." And what time would old Santy Claus come? Mama smiled a secret smile and said, "Nobody knows."

"Bet Santy knows."

"No, not even Santy knows. Sometimes he's late, and sometimes he's later."

So I asked to hear all about old Santy Claus again like we did every year. And Mama told it, but she left out some of the little things, so I had to remind her to put them in. And she did. Then me and Junie hunched up on the couch on our knees and looked out the window straight up at the cold white stars. Here old Santy Claus would come streaking right through those stars, leaping over the frosty lumps of mountaintops. I shivered with excitement.

"It ain't Christmas without Daddy," Junie said, but nobody else had anything to say about that.

Instead, Mama told us, "Go warm your fannies now. And hop inna bed."

We did as we were told because it was Christmas Eve.

We undressed and stood around the heatin' stove in our homemade petticoats, warming our front sides, then our backsides, real good so we could carry some of the heat with us to the cold bedroom in back.

I had a notion that Junie did not believe Santy would come flying over the mountaintops in his goody wagon. She didn't talk about it, but you could tell she was just going along like her and Mama were pulling a good joke on me. But Junie would see.

We danced across the cold floor, trying not to freeze our feet. Junie scrambled into her bed and I into the other, beneath a pile of hillbilly quilts Mama made with her own hands. I knew Mama would be snuggling up to me soon. I scrunched up in a knot and closed my eyes. I had learned to will myself to dream about anything I wanted to dream about. I could dream about the rose room or about seeing Buddy for the first time when he was a puppy and licked my face. One of my favorite dreams was of Poppy and Granny. We hadn't seen Granny since Daddy's funeral, and Poppy since summer. I missed them.

But tonight I would dream of Santy Claus and his sack of toys, especially the doll Mama wrote him about—a doll with black hair and a bottle to feed her with, like a real baby. I knew only a few people with black hair. Sometimes you saw them in the movies, and the Jew doctor we knew at the coal camp was dark all over. Mama said he had come to Clancy Valley to doctor on miners' children because he was running away from old Hitler and he wanted to be so far back in the sticks he could never be found.

One time he rubbed my hair and said, "These mountain children . . . so fair, such blue eyes." He smiled when he said it. I liked him.

In the icy bedroom I dreamed of Santy Claus. I knew he would come tonight because Mama said he would. She never lied to us. But I couldn't hold the dream in my head. Something kept slipping in at the sides. It would sweep over my dreams like a shadow and make me half awake, so that it wasn't a good dream so much as a wish.

I came awake and I knew then why my dream was so dark. It was Mama crying. All curled up to her back, I could feel her body heaving with great gulping sobs, and I could hear the choking intake of her breath like deep rumblings in your belly at school, when you tell them to hush and they won't. I could tell Mama didn't want to be crying and she was trying to be still about it.

My mama, who knew everything, was crying. I had to think about that. I didn't know what to say or do. I could only wonder what made her take on so. I was wide awake then, and whether you want them to or not, things come to you when you're wide awake, especially in an ice-cold bedroom where you can see your breath. I could look sideways out the window and see a mountain shutting out the sky, looming over us like a giant monster. I could hear Junie breathing and I could hear Mama crying like she was lost forever. I listened for Santy, but didn't hear a thing.

It came to me real slow. Maybe Santy wasn't coming a'tall. Maybe that's why Mama was crying. Maybe she knew all the time he couldn't find us since we moved to Sweet Creek Holler, or maybe you had to have the coal-company tickets to pay him. Or maybe you needed money. And maybe Mama knew we would have no Christmas in the morning.

Yes, it was hard to have Christmas without Daddy. When he was alive, we were all together in the coal camp and you could go to the company store, where you didn't need money. But I had learned since Daddy died that everywhere else in the world you had to have money to buy things. We had only the Social Security check and it was never enough.

It seemed like the mountains closed in on me then. It was the first time of many times to follow that I felt their weight pushing down on me.

Mama was still crying when I drifted away. Somewhere in the black coldness I felt her leave the bed. I heard a noise like a door opening and closing. I felt the presence of Santy Claus in the house. Of course he would come in by the front door! How could he come down a chimney when all we had was that little bitty stovepipe! I smiled, warm and happy. Mama would not need to cry now.

Next thing I knew, Junie was wrapping these pink rabbits around my feet. I looked at her sleepily.

"Santy has come," Junie said. "He brought these new house shoes for you, and this, too."

She wrapped a new housecoat around me.

"Come see."

I rubbed my eyes and followed Junie, stumbling into the warm room. Christmas packages were everywhere—on the floor, on the couch, piled into the corners.

Struck dumb, I started unwrapping the presents Junie handed to me—a tea set, a lunch box, paper dolls, games, mittens, a snowsuit, red rubber boots, socks, shoes, a locket, a store-bought petticoat, a flannel nightgown, a teddy bear, and a black-headed baby doll with a bottle to feed her with. I cuddled her. My baby was more beautiful than I could have imagined her. I was lost with her and my happiness for ever so long before I became aware of voices in the kitchen room—happy Christmas voices. I tucked the baby in my new housecoat and wandered forth out of a dream.

Poppy and Granny were sitting at the kitchen table, drinking whiskey. Their faces crinkled with smiles when I showed myself.

"What in the world you got there, Ginny Carol?" Granny said, like she was as surprised as all get-out.

She about toppled out of her chair and Poppy caught her.

"Santy come last night," I managed to say. "Santy Claus over the mountaintops."

I thought Poppy had something in his eye then. He snorted and turned away from me, so I couldn't tell for sure. Granny hugged me tight and said she loved me. Mama bent down to reach in the oven and brought out biscuits piping hot. The look on her face was better than anything. She was wearing a new dress and all her tears were gone.

I climbed on Poppy's lap, and he held me tight against him, resting his chin on the top of my head.

"Do you love poor ole Poppy?"

Yeah, right then I loved poor ole Poppy and poor ole Granny and the whole poor ole world.

8

That spring there was a trial for Donald Struthers in Coaltown that lasted three days. Mama went every day, but she wouldn't let me and Junie go until the last day. Then it was only because a lawyer told her to bring us and let us sit beside her in court so the jury could see us and feel sorry for us losing our daddy and all.

Coaltown was a bustling, crowded little town with one main street, which followed the river and the natural curve of the mountain bases. Cars were parked ever whichaway and the Black and White Transit hauled people in and out of the hollers to do their business. There was a bank and three movie houses, a post office, two drugstores, a Ben Franklin, some clothing stores, and some hardware and furniture stores, and some stores I didn't know what they were. Then there was the courthouse sitting tall and dark against a big, steep cliff jutting right out into the middle of town. The courthouse was made out of rocks, too, and looked like a part of the mountain, except for the clock in the tower.

There were folks from everywhere crowding into the courtroom. The men wore overalls and T-shirts, their faces pinched into serious frowns, all blue-eyed and blond, with wads of tobacco in their mouths. They stood around the walls with their hands in their back pockets and spit tobacco juice out the windows. The women wore faded-out feed-sack dresses and juggled babies on their hips. Some of them nursed their babies right there in front of the judge and lawyers and everybody, without any expression on their faces that you could read. They all looked wore out, with their blue eyes pale and hollow. Their bare arms sagged with used-up skin, and you couldn't tell how old anybody was because everybody looked old.

Poppy came in and sat down beside me. He patted me on the head and I was proud of him looking as dignified and dressed up as the lawyers. He had on a three-piece pin-striped suit in gray and black, with a gray hat to match, and he was wearing wing-tipped shoes exactly like Clark Gable wore in a movie. I sat up straighter and glanced at Mama. She was the prettiest woman in the room in her pink dress Poppy and Granny bought her for Christmas. She could have passed for sixteen, with her hair all fluffy and gold as corn. A stranger might have thought she was from Bristol or somewhere, instead of Sweet Creek Holler, Virginia.

I didn't understand a thing that happened except when the jury came in and said, "Guilty." Half the people in court cried, and the other half laughed and slapped each other on the back. Mama and Poppy just turned and looked at each other, then hugged real tight, and I saw that Mama's cheeks were wet. I got one good look at Donald Struthers. He was old and bald, and his head sagged down on his chest.

When the Coaltown newspaper was published that week, it said Donald Struthers's defense was weak because he couldn't give a shred of evidence that Jed Shortt was trying to steal from him. Three witnesses for my daddy said he was helping them change a flat tire in the dark in front of Struthers's gas station. They had their own spare, so they sure didn't need to steal a tire from Struthers like he said. But Struthers came out and started shooting wild, and my daddy got hit.

When Mama read that in the paper, she did something I never knew her to do before or since. She got all dressed up and went visiting our neighbors up and down the holler. And she took me and Junie with her. She visited the Moores, the Jenkinses, the Ratliffs, the Looneys, the Purvises, and others, and everybody made her welcome. At each house she read aloud the account of Daddy's death, because, as she told me and Junie, some of our neighbors couldn't read for their own selves. Her voice shook a little as she read, because she wasn't used to reading to anybody but me and Junie.

Then she would say, "I just wanted everybody to know that Jed Shortt, my late husband and these girls' daddy, never stole a thing in his life, and it says here in black and white that he was innocent of stealing from Donald Struthers."

"Why, Miz Shortt," all our neighbors said, "we never believed a thing like that in the first place."

When summer came again, Christine, Tildy, Lou Jean, Junie, and me played in the wild like young animals. There was a fire watchtower at the head of

Sweet Creek Holler on the mountaintop, which was never manned. The five of us would climb to the top and look out over Sweet Creek Holler and Hoot Owl Holler, Dry Creek Holler, and far-off hollers we didn't know the names of. We played Skin the Cat on rails ninety feet above the earth. Of course, our mamas didn't know where we were or they would have whooped us good. We would say we were going picnicking, and we would sure enough carry picnic lunches with spiced ham and tomato sandwiches, side meat stuffed into biscuits, green apples, raspberries, sometimes fudge or fried apple pies, and Kool-Aid. Then we took our food to the top landing of the tower and ate, dropping our crumbs for the birds.

We chased each other up and down the steps of the tower, marveling at the magnificent height, the view, the miracle of steel that perched this giant so high on the highest hill and made us happy for a day. We felt no fear of falling, and if I thought about it at all I would just shiver, then laugh in joyous abandon, and scamper up another flight.

The slate dump behind the Clancys' was another play spot our mamas didn't know about. We figured out that if we cut a grapevine above the cliff we could swing out over the danger of the jagged, burning rocks far below. We never slipped, or even stumbled, on returning to the cliff, because we did not think it was possible.

One of those days at the slate dump stood out from all others and came to me again and again at odd moments in the future. It was one of those moments you know on the spot that you will remember forever. You can see yourself as an old gray-headed lady poking around in your dusty memories and up pops this one: The yellow jackets were buzzing around the wildflowers, and the rocks were so hot they burned our feet. Christine and Tildy were at a distance from the dump, picking black-eyed Susans. A hummingbird was sucking nectar from a clover bloom, and Lou Jean's sweaty little hand with its broken-off nails suddenly gripped my arm.

"Oh, look at her, Ginny!" Lou Jean whispered breathlessly.

My sister's brown body was flying into the sun above the slate dump.

"Look at Junie!"

Junie's feet flew like wings beating against the empty air, and her hair stood on end with the speed of her flight.

"She *can't* fall, Ginny!" Lou Jean went on. "Don't you see, she *can't* fall! We are special, you and me and Junie. We will live forever!"

I shivered with excitement. Yes, it was true. Death and pain always came to others, but we were unafraid, because we were going to live forever!

·   ·   ·

Then there were the Saturday nights. Just about everybody in the holler listened to the Grand Ole Opry live from Nashville, Tennessee, on the radio. Me and Junie usually went to bed before it was over, but the radios played on through the night up and down the valley. The sounds of twanging guitars, banjos, and fiddles playing all the hillbilly favorites echoed through the dark hills.

Junie didn't like to sing as much as Lou Jean and I did. The two of us knew all the Opry regulars and most all the words to their songs. Lou Jean would sneak off with me into the hills, where we would pick a cliff for our stage and sing our hearts out to the trees, our audience. I was getting to be almost as good as Lou Jean. When she taught me to harmonize with her, I thought for sure the two of us were headed for stardom.

At the first of each month, the Social Security check would come in the mail and we would go to the movies. Mama decided that summer that we were old enough to go by ourselves; so Junie and me would dress up in our best dresses, walk to the mouth of the holler, catch the Black and White Transit to Coaltown to see a show, and have a bag of popcorn and a bottle of pop. Sometimes we went on Saturday and watched Roy Rogers, my favorite, who played at the Glenwood one Saturday of every month. But sometimes we went on Sunday to see a musical—maybe Howard Keel and Kathryn Grayson, or Doris Day. We liked Judy Canova, too. We could carry on over a good movie for a whole month, acting out all the parts, and remembering most of the lines and songs.

Once Poppy popped in on a Wednesday and said, "I'm taking my girls to the show." He took us in a taxicab to see *Snow White and the Seven Dwarfs*. Poppy didn't know we had outgrown fairy tales, but we acted like we were real impressed. Later, he bought us a bottle of pop, loaded our hands with Milky Ways, and sent us home in a taxi.

"Tell your mama I'm going to bring her that refrigerator tomorrow," he said.

But we didn't see or hear from him again for months. We still had to use canned milk, and even the smallest jar of mayonnaise went bad before we could use it up. We had to buy butter from the Ratliffs every day. It sure would have been nice to have a refrigerator, but that was just the way Poppy was, we reckoned.

One time when the Social Security check came, Christine, Tildy, and Lou Jean decided they wanted to go to the show with us. And lo and behold, their mama let 'em. It was on the way home that day that Tildy cocked her mouth crooked and said, "Here's lookin' atcha, kid." And from that day to this, I reckon, you couldn't shut her up. I always wondered what might have happened to Tildy if she hadn't gone with us that day. Would she still be speechless? It was like a cloudburst, and for weeks after, she was the talk of the holler. Folks said, "You know that little Ratliff gal finally found her tongue and now she won't let it rest."

When I asked her, "Tildy, how come you never talked before?" she answered me, " 'Cause I didn't have nothing to say before."

Claude Estep, a miner who lived up in the head of the holler, drove his pickup truck past our house on his way to and from work. He was always delivering messages to people along the way, and one evening he stopped at our house. Mrs. Brown, my teacher, wanted Mama and Junie and me to come to her house for supper on Friday evening. Mama dressed up in her best dress. It was blue with pretty white spiderwebs all over it. Daddy got it for her the Christmas before he died. She had rolled her hair in tin strips earlier in the day, and it fell out all curly and fluffy around her face like milkweed. Then she put on lipstick and powdered her nose so it wouldn't shine. She smelled and looked like spring. Me and Junie dressed in our good dresses and put on our shoes.

Mr. Brown came to get us in his pickup truck. It seemed like he couldn't take his eyes off Mama as he drove us to his white house down on Highway 460 by the Levisa River. But when Mrs. Brown saw how pretty Mama was, she turned real red, then she got that tight-lipped expression and didn't say much. Then she said less and less. Mama didn't notice at first, because she was so excited about going out on a real invitation to a teacher's house. She wanted to make friends with Mrs. Brown. She talked and laughed more than any time I could remember since Daddy died, and her cheeks were rosy and her eyes bright.

But Mrs. Brown didn't talk back. She just watched and listened while Mr. Brown and Mama talked, and didn't even notice me and Junie were in the room. When she served up supper, she did it with a slam and a bang of pots and pans and dishes. Mama all of a sudden got quiet, too, and the roses left her cheeks. Her eyes got that fine little worry line between them, and she started watching the clock.

As soon as we finished eating, Mrs. Brown insisted her husband drive us home and she would go along for the ride. She sat between Mama and her man in the cab, so that me and Junie had to ride in the back. Though Mrs. Brown was always polite enough to me after that, she was never quite the same.

9

The beginning of the second grade was just like the beginning of the first grade, except for two things: one was Junior Longridge, a new boy and the only boy in the world worth fooling with. He had that mysterious rarity called curly black hair—black as coal—and his eyes were sorta blue-green like pictures of the ocean. He had straight white teeth grinning at you out of a smooth tan face. On that first day we were lined up on the wraparound porch at school getting our yearly typhoid shots, when he walked up and started talking to me. I'll declare I didn't even feel the needle and the public-health nurse had to tell me to move on and get out of the way. Junior could render you speechless just by looking at you.

The second difference was that Lou Jean went away to Coaltown to the seventh grade that year. I missed her, but in a way I was glad she wouldn't be around to get all of Junior's attention. She was getting so pretty, nobody could resist her. The second best-looking girl in Sweet Creek, I thought, was Junie, and she made it clear to me that she was in fifth grade and not a'tall interested in any li'l ole second-grade boy, no matter how cute he was. The rest of us girls ranged in looks from plain ugly to average, and I figured I was about as average as the rest, so I fancied I might become Junior's girlfriend.

Christine went away to Coaltown to school that year, too, but Tildy was with me in Mrs. Brown's second grade along with Junior, Susie Ruth, and part of last year's crop of first-graders. Clover Weed finally had made it to the third grade. Buddy came back to school with me for a while. But after a few weeks in the second grade he decided his education was complete. He started staying home with Mama.

Junior took an interest in Buddy, and I found I could brag about him chewing up on Clover Weed. Junior would get so tickled he would hold his sides laughing, but then he would always walk off to join his pals. So I learned that fall how it was to go pining after something you can't have, and all the wishing in the world won't make it yours. Still, I never stopped wishing.

Lou Jean's mama got sick in October and was in the hospital for a couple of weeks. Nit was so drunk half the time and so easygoing the other half, he didn't seem to mind what Lou Jean did. She was free to play with me all she wanted to.

One day we were just resting and dreaming in October's golden leaves on the hillside below her house and I said to her, "What kind of car you gonna buy when we get rich and famous in Nashville, Lou Jean?"

"What?" Lou Jean's pouty pink lips made an O.

"Yeah, you want a Ford, a Chevy, or what?"

"Oh, heck, Ginny." Her voice was soft. "I been thinking on those dreams. You know that's all they are, little girls' dreams. We're growing up now."

"Dreams, my hind foot! I'm gonna be a famous singer! That's a fact! And so are you. We can sing good, Lou. As good as anybody on the radio."

"Ginny, we got to quit talking like that. God can strike us voiceless in a second if'n we brag."

"Brag! Gosh, Lou Jean, God gave us our voices. Don't you think we're good?"

"What I think don't count. We shouldn't make ourselves out to be more'n we are."

"Well, I ain't. God don't care, Lou Jean. Not if he's really God."

"Ginny, sometimes I think he listens to us talking—well, I know he does—'specially proud talking like that, and he says, 'I'll just show that girl who's the boss.'"

"Aw, Lou . . ."

"I mean it. Mama told me he does. We shouldn't think too much of our own selves. We're just little ants to him—bugs."

"Naw . . ."

"Yeah, bugs. And he burns bad bugs in hell's fire."

"Then God is a monster," I said angrily.

"Don't say that!" Lou Jean's face grew pale. "Mama says we'll account for every idle word. God sees and knows all, and he will punish us!"

"Well, I don't believe God throws people into fire, Lou Jean! It would take an awful creature to do a thing like that."

"We ask for it with our wicked ways," she said with much feeling in her voice. "Now, please, Ginny, don't say anything else to offend God."

I fell silent. We walked to the cliff overlooking the slate dump without another word to offend God.

"You first, Ginny," Lou Jean said sweetly.

Lou Jean was always putting others ahead of herself.

I grabbed the vine and backed up far behind the cliff. "Here I go!"

I pushed off and felt myself flying over the edge of the cliff and far, far into the air, over the burning rubble far below. "Whoo . . . eee! I'm king of the hills!"

The vine brought me back. I groped with my toes for the cliff's edge and Lou Jean grabbed me to safety, laughing.

"That's what I'm going to be, Lou Jean!" I said, with the wind still in my brain. "A trapeze artist! A flying trapeze artist!"

Lou Jean took hold of the vine, backed up far, and swung. "Flying . . . flying . . . flying trapeze artist!" she yelled into the wind.

Over the burning rocks she laughed, the sun blotting her out of sight for a moment. I shivered deliciously. Then the flying feet came back, groping for the cliff, and I grabbed for Lou Jean. There was a crackle in the trees above me, and to my horror the vine suddenly slipped through the branches and through my fingers. Lou Jean was left dangling below the edge of the cliff.

She screamed. The vine slipped again, and I clutched frantically at what was left of it.

"Hold me! Hold me!" Lou Jean screamed. "Pull me up, Ginny!"

"Lordy, mercy," I cried in desperation. Looking up, I could now see the other end of the vine was loose from the tree. The only thing holding Lou Jean out of the jagged hot slate far below was me. My own hands, clinging to the vine, were white with strain. I fell to my knees on the cliff and pulled with all my strength, but Lou Jean was too heavy. I could not get her above the edge of the cliff.

"Please hold on! Please don't let me fall!"

"Help! Help!" I screamed.

The vine was cutting into my hands, and I was being pulled toward the edge of the cliff by Lou Jean's weight.

Then all of a sudden a great big person was looming over me. He bent down, took the vine from my hands and pulled Lou Jean up easily, grabbed her by the shoulders, and hauled her to safety. It was Josh Clancy.

"The only time you ever see Josh Clancy out on foot is in the fall time," Christine had told us that first day. "He goes to check on the fire to see it don't spread to the dry leaves."

Well, praise God for the fall time.

Me and Lou Jean hugged each other and cried. Josh stood over us, breathing hard, and his whole body shook.

"I ought to thrash you both!" he said, like he was mad as the devil.

We were crying so hard we couldn't say a word.

"Of all the damn idiotic stunts I have ever seen pulled by two fool kids, this one takes the prize!"

Lou Jean looked up at him. "Please, please don't tell my mama," she begged, sobbing.

"Don't you know you could have been killed?" he said more quietly.

Killed? Not us. But we nodded.

"Well, this is Clancy land," he said, and took a deep breath. "And I want you to stay away from this dump. If I ever see either one of you or any other child anywhere near here again, I will get the sheriff and have you arrested. Do you hear?"

We nodded again.

"You sure you understand?"

"Yeah," I said, wiping my nose on my sleeve.

Then Josh Clancy picked up the vine where it lay on the cliff and tossed it over into the slate dump.

"Now go home!"

He stalked away from us. I watched him through tears, so it was hard to say for sure what I really saw that day. I know what I think I saw. A little ways away from us, he turned back around and stood looking at us with his hands on his hips, and I'd just about swear there were two little girls with him, one on either side—two little yella-headed girls in white sailor dresses. Then they all three walked away.

"Did you see 'em, Lou Jean?"

"See what?" she asked, blubbering.

"I don't know. Did you see somebody with Josh?"

"No."

I said no more.

We stumbled down the hill, and Lou Jean couldn't stop crying.

"The slate dump is just like hell," she sobbed. "And I about fell in."

"You didn't fall." I patted her shoulder.

It seemed funny having to reach up and comfort a big girl who seemed younger than me.

"What's a flying trapeze artist, Ginny?"

"It's a circus performer that flies on a rope above the crowd."

"Then that's it. It was a sign I was too proud."

I couldn't stand any more of that talk.

"Horse hockey!" I hollered.

I didn't tell anybody but Junie about Lou Jean's narrow escape on the cliff, and as far as I know, Lou Jean didn't tell anybody. Junie's eyes got round as a clock and she appeared to be frightened. Then I told her about the ghost girls and she got real serious.

"I wonder if they're really ghosts," she said after a spell. "I don't really believe in ghosts, do you, Ginny?"

"I never used to, but I don't know now . . ."

"I think it's somebody we used to know," Junie said.

"What!"

"Oh, I don't know. It's just a thought."

"Well, what'd you mean?"

"Nothing. Forget it. I guess they are ghosts."

And she wouldn't talk about it again for a long time.

10

It was a hard, cold winter. Mama bundled me up so I could hardly move to send me off to school. She would hand me my dinner bucket packed with two side-meat biscuits, and fruit when we had it. Fruit was hard to come by in winter, and cost lots of money. She would tell Junie to "be sure Ginny eats it all." Then she would hug us both and stand in the door with a worried look on her face while we trudged off to school.

Buddy would wag his tail at us, and curl up by the heatin' stove. He was getting to be a smart dog.

But lo and behold one January morning along came a big yella school bus poking up the road all the way to the head of the holler, where it turned and picked up all the children on the way back down. It stopped right in front of our gate.

"Praise the Lord!" Mama said, happy as could be. "Now my girls won't have to walk in the cold no more."

Life was easier. We didn't have to get up so early, or dress so warm, or come home in the evenings plum wore out.

Me and Junior Longridge were assigned to water-bucket duty together. That meant Junior hauled up the bucket of water out of the well and I dipped it out to the children in cups made out of notebook paper, making sure nobody drank out of the dipper. Junior always stood beside me and talked to me. It was the best part of the day.

"What'd ole Santy bring you, Ginny?" he'd say.

Or, "Done your 'rithmetic, Ginny?"

Or, "How's ole Buddy, Ginny?"

But slow, without me hardly noticing, the conversation changed.

"Look at that pink ribbon in Susie Ruth's hair. Ain't it pretty?"

"Look at Susie Ruth's little bitty feet. Ain't they cute?"

"Look at Susie Ruth's pitcher of Old Man Winter. Kain't she draw good?"

I couldn't help noticing after a while. And when I sat with Junie at lunchtime trying to choke down my biscuits, I couldn't help noticing how Junior showed off and danced around Susie Ruth.

"Ain't he silly, Junie?"

"Yeah, he's sweet on Susie Ruth, ain't he?"

It was true.

The winter grew even harder and colder. It was still snowing in March. I developed a cold and couldn't shake it. Even though Mrs. Brown took pity on me and moved me closer to the heatin' stove, I still couldn't stay warm. My teeth chattered all the time. Mama made me eat all I could hold, but I just kept falling off. I was also wetting the bed again and having nightmares.

One night I dreamed that shadows darkened the hills and the sky was a deep purple over the narrow valley. I was alone in the woods. A vulture swept down over me, brushing my hair with its wing tips. Someone was crying so sadly it like to have melted my heart away, and it was coming from a dark hole in the rich black earth.

I knew it was Lou Jean crying.

"Where are you, Lou Jean? I'll help you. Where are you?"

"Oh, Ginny, Ginny, I'm lost."

"Where are you, Lou Jean?"

I groped across the face of the mountain. Darkness was getting thick. A great beast of fear stalked me through the strange, dark woods. And sadness so deep I was filled with grief.

Then there was the sound of many clocks ticking away the precious minutes of the night—and yes, of my life. They filled my head with a great clamor. *Tick-tock. Tick-tock.* All ten thousand at once crowding into my brain, and I started to cry, too.

"Lou Jean!"

But there was no answer.

They will all go away, I thought. Today and tomorrow will tick away into yesterday, and I will lose them all—Mama, Junie, Lou Jean, Poppy, Granny, Buddy—they will all leave me—just like Daddy did.

"Lou Jean!" I screamed into the vast, empty blackness of the hole in the mountainside. But Lou Jean's weeping echoed across the hills, the sky, the valley, and was lost.

"Wake up, Ginny! Wake up!"

"*Lou Jean!*"

"You're dreaming. It's just a dream, Gin-Gin. Wake up now."

"Mama!"

"Another nightmare, Gin-Gin?" Mama held me close.

"Oh, Mama, Lou Jean was in a black hole. I couldn't find her, and I thought everybody I love will leave me like this someday."

"Just a dream, little Gin, just a dream. Mama will always be here."

"Oh, Mama, I love Lou Jean!"

"I know you do."

"But she fell in a hole."

"It was just a dream."

"But something is wrong with Lou Jean."

"Why do you say that?"

"She's lost, Mama."

"No, she's home snug in bed."

"No, she's lost."

"Ginny, Ginny, you think too much. Tomorrow we'll go to the doctor's."

The rest of the night, Mama held me warm in her arms.

Ever after, Mama said it seemed like it was meant

for her to take me to the doctor's the next day because of what came of it. We had finished up at the doctor's and were just going into the Coaltown Rexall when here came Poppy up the street.

"Olivia! Ginny!"

"Hidy, Poppy." I managed a grin for him, though my head hurt awful.

"Hello, Taylor. I just had to bring Ginny Carol to Coaltown to see the doctor."

"Well, what in the world?" he said. "Come on in here and let me buy you a cup of coffee."

We settled into a high-back booth. The drugstore was dark and warm and empty. I felt drowsy. I snuggled against Mama.

"Two cups of coffee and some hot cocoa for my girl here," Poppy said to the waitress.

"How's Sadie?" Mama said.

"Sadie's in Roanoke getting dried out," Poppy said sadly. "I reckon liquor's gonna kill her yet."

"That's too bad," Mama said. "I thought she was going to be all right, till Jed died."

"Yeah, that done it. But now tell me, what's wrong with my girl Ginny?"

"Doctor says she's run down something awful."

"Run down?"

"Yeah. She ain't getting her vitamins and minerals and stuff she needs. Doctor gave me a list of stuff to buy here." Mama pulled a piece of paper from her coat pocket. "He checked the most important ones 'cause I told him I can't afford 'em all."

Poppy took the list.

"Cod-liver oil, vitamin C, iron—how come she ain't getting this stuff in her food, Olivia?"

Mama's face turned red, like it was her fault.

"Food cost so much, Taylor. I buy what I can for my girls. You know I wouldn't let 'em starve. But oranges and fresh vegetables and liver—things like that—I'd have to go to Coaltown to the A&P and get a taxi to bring me home, and I'd have to have cash. John Looney ain't got much but dry goods and canned stuff in his store, but he gives me credit. And also, Taylor, a lot of things won't save without a refrigerator, you know."

It was Poppy's turn to get red.

"I know it, Olivia. What *do* you feed these girls in the wintertime?"

"Well, the stuff I canned last summer is long gone. We eat soup beans and side meat, and taters and corn bread and canned milk. We eat milk gravy and biscuits for breakfast. Sometimes we get canned sausage, but it's awful high."

Poppy didn't say a word for the longest, then he looked at me with pity and said, "She's so pale, and so little. You hungry, little Ginny?"

"Not much."

"Want a hamburger?"

"What do they taste like?"

"They're rich," he grinned, and called the waitress. "Three hamburgers with everything on 'em but the dishrag."

Mama and the waitress laughed out loud.

"And three big glasses of orange juice," Poppy went on. "And take this list." Poppy handed the list to the waitress. "And bring me everything on it."

Mama took off her coat and relaxed. The tight worry lines were gone from her face. The hamburger was hot and juicy, and filled an empty place in me I didn't even know was there. It seemed like my belly had always been waiting for a hamburger. Later, Poppy packed us off to home in a taxicab and said not to worry about a thing. He was gonna take care of his little Ginny.

At home I snuggled into bed, warm and content. But later I felt guilty about the hamburger, because Junie didn't get one. I didn't tell her about it. How can you tell a sister you love she missed out on the best-tasting food in the world? Mama didn't tell her either, but when she served up beans again for supper that night, she hugged Junie like she was apologizing.

The next day, two strange men showed up in a pickup truck with a refrigerator loaded on it.

"Where you want it, Miz Shortt?"

It was a big white Frigidaire with ice trays and a vegetable crisper. Nobody else in the holler had a refrigerator as nice as ours. Four big pokes of groceries came with it, including fresh vegetables, fruit, and fresh meat. Mama was so happy she cried.

The next week, another big poke of groceries came from Poppy, then a smaller one the week after. Then we heard no more from Poppy for months.

One night Mama and Mrs. Ratliff cooked up a big batch of beef stew and set off down the holler with it in a pot between them.

"Where's she going to?" I asked Junie.

"To the Weeds' house."

"The Weeds? What in the world for?"

" 'Cause their little baby girl died, Ginny."

"Oh."

"Yeah, she was only three years old. This one was named Pansy."

Pansy—another flower.

"Doctor said she died of malnutrition," Junie went on.

A big lump came up in my throat. That was the same word the doctor used when he was talking to Mama about me. It meant little Pansy Weed didn't get enough to eat, and I guess she didn't have a Poppy.

11

Spring did arrive in 1950, though we thought it never would. It brought warmth and health back to me. Mama worked hard planting a huge garden and making plans to can twice as much of everything for the next cold winter. And summer did come, too, in spite of all the cold and sorrow of winter. The feel of the warm earth beneath my feet was a fine thing. I hung around with Lou Jean all I could. She was the sweetest girl in the world, and when we were together I managed to forget the terrible dream about her. After all, as Mama said, it was only a dream.

I entered third grade that fall, and Junie entered sixth grade. Mrs. Simpson got a telephone that year at her house, and everybody had to go see it and talk and listen on it. But the telephone lines hadn't been strung up yet in the holler where we lived. It was rumored some doctor in Coaltown had bought a television set, but his reception was so bad on account of the mountains that nobody else wanted to buy one. Everybody declared television would never take the place of the radio. But still, we thought the mountains of Virginia were really making progress.

I made all Es in school that year (E meaning excellent), and so did Junie, though that was nothing new to her. Junior Longridge sometimes asked me to help him with his arithmetic, and of course I did. Every once in a while he gave me a sucker for helping him, but that was about as far as our relationship went. Tildy was barely keeping up in school, so I helped her, too.

Then the third grade was over, summer arrived again and was gone again just like that. The fourth grade approached.

That September, when Junie went away to school in Coaltown, a wonderful thing happened. There was a library at Coaltown High School, and she could bring home books for free. Even though we read mostly to our own selves quiet, we still loved to curl up to Mama on the couch and have her read to us before bedtime. We went through the Laura Ingalls Wilder books that way, *Lassie Come Home, Heidi, A Girl of the Limberlost, Trail of the Lonesome Pine, Lorna Doone,* and many more. To her own self, Mama read a lot of Poe, Jane Austen, Dickens, Hardy, and the

Brontës. Then one day she asked Junie to bring home some English grammar books.

"I'm going to learn to talk better," she announced. "Maybe it'll help me get a good job some-day."

It had got so Mama never went out of the house anymore. Every time she did, somebody started something. Every married woman watched her like a hawk. It was because she was so pretty and a widow. Old fat Mrs. Moore was the worst gossip of all. Seemed like all she ever did was sit on her porch and holler personal questions to people as they went by. If you didn't answer, she made up her own answers. And if you did answer, she still made up her own answers. Then the next person to come down the road got an earful of whatever she found out from the last person. Everybody knew what the old vulture was up to, but they still listened to her stories every chance they got. Some folks went to see her 'specially to find out what sleazy happenings were underway. Gossip was the chief form of entertainment, and it was amazing what mean things people wanted to believe about their neighbors.

So Mama just stayed indoors and got lost in her books. Not even Mrs. Moore could make something out of nothing. Me and Junie stayed out of Mrs. Moore's way most of the time, but sometimes you just couldn't help running into her. She showed up for every event, be it a candy party, a baby shower, a revival, a quilting—there she was looking and listening, her nose twitching with curiosity.

A new family moved into a shack up on the hill down below Copperhead Bridge. They were the Mayfields, and Dora Faye was my age. We started hanging around together all the time and playing like. Most of the time we were Anne and Jeannette, two Hollywood starlets who had everything. I was Anne, a brunette loved by Lash LaRue, and Dora Faye was Jeannette, a blonde loved by Guy Madison. Dora Faye read *True Story* and all the movie magazines besides, so she could come up with some of the best imaginings I ever did hear tell of.

At school I started writing love stories. They were so sad Dora Faye would read them and cry, then pass them around to Susie Ruth, Tildy, and others, and they would cry, too. Dora Faye, Susie Ruth, Tildy, and me became best friends, and sat together under an old persimmon tree every day at lunchtime, swapping secrets and dreams.

"Let's be friends forever," I said one day when we were all feeling about as mellow as one of those old ripe persimmons.

"Let's do," Susie Ruth cooed, and took my hand.

We all joined hands in a circle.

"Let's promise not ever to forget each other," Tildy said.

"And never let no boy come between us," Susie Ruth said.

That was easy enough for her to say.

"And always stick up for each other," I said. "I'll write it all down and we'll sign it just like a contract."

"You get the best ideas, Ginny," Dora Faye said.

I was tickled to death. We all smiled at each other. After lunch, I wrote up the contract instead of doing my arithmetic, and passed it around for the others to sign. And nobody broke it, not for a long time anyway.

Secretly I considered Lou Jean my best friend forever, but she was getting away from me. Five years older, she had found other interests—boys being one of them. Still, she was sweet and helpful to me, and never acted like I wasn't wanted when I tried to hang around her. I didn't like to go to her house because her mama scared the fool out of me, but I did go sometimes if it was the only way I could get to see Lou Jean.

Then she fell in love with Will Jenkins. That's when she really got away from me. She was growing up. In fact, everybody was growing up, and I felt a strange longing to hold on to the present. Sometimes

I could hear all those clocks ticking away even when I wasn't dreaming.

Next thing I knew, I was finishing fifth grade. Me and Tildy, Susie Ruth, and Dora Faye were all eleven years old, Junie was fourteen, and Christine and Lou Jean were sixteen.

Part Two

12

It was the last part of May and the first day of summer vacation. Junie told me Lou Jean's boyfriend, Will, went away to the army, so I fancied it would be a good time to visit Lou. I hadn't seen her to have a good talk in a month of Sundays.

She smiled at me funny when I went in, and old Mrs. Purvis just grunted. Lou Jean was sewing something or other, and I sat down beside her.

"You glad school's out, Lou Jean?" I said.

"Yeah."

"Me, too."

Then I couldn't think of another thing to say, so I just sat there and watched her. I got the feeling something was wrong. She bent low over her sewing, her light hair covering her face so that only the tip of her nose could be seen from the side. She was real little for sixteen, and at the moment she seemed even littler. She was drawn up like a kitten curled in a knot.

Mrs. Purvis, standing in the open doorway with her hands on her hips and staring out toward the road, appeared to be about seven feet tall. She was wearing a dress the color of pickles, which oddly matched her face.

Directly Mrs. Purvis said, "Somebody coming."

Lou Jean lifted her face to look out, but her mama filled the open doorway. Her fingers trembled when her mama spoke, and her gaze fell back to her sewing as Mrs. Purvis turned to her.

The old woman's eyes got narrow and her sour face turned cruel as she looked at her daughter. "It's a man," she said in a thick whisper. "Ain't you gonna jump up and meet him?"

"No," Lou Jean said, turning red.

Mrs. Purvis laughed. "Thought you would."

The man knocked.

"Hidy do," Mrs. Purvis said as she turned back to the open door. "What can I do fer ye?"

"Good afternoon," the man said cheerfully. "Madam, may I take a few moments of your time?"

"Hmmm . . ." the big woman mumbled and motioned him in.

"Good afternoon," he said to me and Lou Jean.

We nodded as Mrs. Purvis pointed to a chair for the stranger. He was selling *The Book of Knowledge*. He spoke with a Yankee accent and he had these lumps all over his face. What he said about the books was interesting, but even more interesting were those lumps on his face. They were raised places that looked like mosquito bites, but they weren't red and he didn't scratch them, so they couldn't be mosquito bites. Besides, mosquitoes don't bite you on the face; that's too handy. They crawl into that little crease behind your knee, or on the inside of your elbow. They like bony places too, like your anklebone or your wristbone, where it hurts to scratch. I was experienced when it came to mosquito bites.

Mrs. Purvis settled into a rocking chair and listened to his spiel.

"You don't say," she mumbled ever once in a while when he stressed a particularly interesting point about his books. "That so?"

Lou Jean peeped up once to look at the man's face, then went back to her work.

When the man finished his sales pitch, an uncomfortable silence followed. He looked from mother to daughter to me, expecting something. Lou Jean was still curled up in a knot. He took a handkerchief from his pocket and wiped the sweat from his neck.

"Hot," he said.

"How much?" Mrs. Purvis asked.

"What?" the man said, looking at Lou Jean.

"How much fer your books?"

"Oh! Only $27.50."

"Ain't got it."

"Well, how about five dollars down and five dollars a month?"

"Naw, reckon not."

"Oh, well." The man got up to go. "I guess I'll . . ."

"But I'll trade with you," Mrs. Purvis interrupted him.

"Trade?"

"Yeah. I'll give you something, you give me something—the books."

"Oh." The man grinned. "You mean like chickens or potatoes or something?"

"No, I mean her." Mrs. Purvis pointed to Lou Jean. "Take my girl with you."

"What! . . . Oh! . . . It's a joke?"

"No, it ain't."

"You can't mean . . . ?"

"That's what I mean. Give me the books and take this sorry girl with you wherever you're going to."

Her face was serious.

The salesman was struck dumb. Lou Jean, trembling, went on with her sewing, sticking her fingers, but she never let out a sound.

"You want something t'boot?" Mrs. Purvis said. "Don't you think she's worth $27.50?"

"But you can't . . ."

"Kain't I?" Lou Jean's mama laughed suddenly, showing big ole gray teeth, not a bit like Nit's and Lou Jean's.

"*No!*" the man shouted.

He glanced at Lou Jean, then at Mrs. Purvis. He gathered up his books, all huffy and puffy.

"Good day!" he said.

"No, I reckon she's not worth $27.50," Mrs. Purvis said.

The man ran out the door.

Lou Jean's hands couldn't go on. They froze at the needle, and she stared down at the garment in her lap, without seeing it. Mrs. Purvis started rocking back and forth fast, mumbling to herself.

I wanted to go home, but I was afraid to move.

Five minutes later the man was standing in the doorway again, finding us all in the same positions as when he left.

"Yeah?" Mrs. Purvis grunted, looking at him. "Forgit something?"

"I . . . I . . ." he couldn't say it.

"Change your mind?" Mrs. Purvis grinned.

He nodded.

"You want my girl then for the books?"

"Only if she wants to go with me," he said, red-faced.

Lou Jean's head shot up and her eyes darted wildly from one face to the other.

"Oh, she wants to go all right, don't you, girl?"

"No!" Lou Jean cried out.

Then she lunged out of her chair, past the man and through the door, and jumped off the porch. I followed her as fast as my skinny legs would carry me. She ran down the hillside and followed the creek upward a ways. The Clancy barn, weathered silver, hung tiredly on the opposite hill like it was about to fall off. She went in the barn, and I started after her.

The Clancys' three old horses blinked stupidly at Lou Jean, then turned to look at me. I backed off. I wasn't about to tangle with no horses. There was one of those half-sawed-off doors I could barely see over, and I had to stand on tiptoe to see her.

"Lou Jean," I said, but she didn't answer.

"Lou Jean!" I said again.

I could see her sitting in a pile of loose hay with a box of kitchen matches in her hand. I saw her take one of the matches and strike it. Then she looked long and hard right into the center of the blue flame.

"Please, Lou Jean," I pleaded.

"Go home, Ginny!" she said in a voice that didn't belong to her. "Let me be!"

It hurt having Lou Jean talk so hateful to me, but then I thought how I would feel if my mama tried to trade me off for a $27.50 set of encyclopedias. I went home.

That was the day the Clancys' barn mysteriously burned down. I didn't tell a soul what I knew about that. Somebody fetched the Coaltown Fire Department, but it was too late. Nearly everybody in the holler turned out to watch that fire—even Mama. I guess only three people stayed away—Mrs. Clancy, Lou Jean, and me—yes, me. I was sick. All the events of the day like to have turned my stomach against me: Lou Jean's face when that ugly old man came back to get her, and the expression she wore when she was looking into that match flame. On top of everything else, some fool saved those horses, and now they were running loose somewhere in the holler. It all scared me so, I was sick.

The next morning, real early, I had to make a trip to the outhouse to upchuck. But there was nothing left to come up. I stood there retching and retching till I thought my liver was coming up. Then I went out in the cool air and leaned my head against a tree. The grass was wet with dew and soothing on my bare feet. It was just barely daylight and a soupy fog lay thick on everything. You couldn't even see the moun-taintops. But you could see the fog curling and crawling over the creek and over the road, and over Copperhead Bridge like a live thing.

Then I heard the funny noise: *Clippity-clop. Clippity-clop.* I looked up the road, and there came the horses, all three running free. My skin prickled. They were young horses again, and happy. And there riding on their backs were the ghost girls, their white sailor dresses and their yella hair floating on the wind. On the third horse was a boy about sixteen years old. The bigger girl and the boy were laughing, but the little girl was clinging to the saddle and was all bent over, seeming about as scared as me.

"Don't give him so much lead, Shirley!" the big girl said. "Show him who is boss!"

But the little girl clung tighter and her eyes turned to me where I stood trembling in the dew and fog. Did Shirley know me? Did her eyes show a spark of recognition? And who was the boy? Why did they show themselves to me on this particular day? It had been four years since I last saw the girls at the slate dump with Josh, and here they were, unchanged, and wearing the same dresses. Yet I was older, taller, smarter.

Then the children vanished, and it was just those nasty horses, old once more and without saddles or riders, running down the middle of the road, splitting the fog.

For a couple of weeks after that, I stayed close to Mama, but I didn't see the horses again. A little at a time, I went out more often. Then I got back into the serious business of being a movie star, horses almost forgotten. It was a hot, sticky day toward the end of June when Mama asked me to go to the store for some blueing.

"You can buy a Pepsi," she promised. So I went.

I met the horses on my return trip. When I first saw them, they were up on the hill chomping grass with their nasty teeth. I was facing death. They saw me right off, but they were clever. They just watched me out of the corner of their evil eyes. As I got closer, they moved down the hill. It was an awful good time to visit with Mrs. Moore, I thought. She was sitting on her porch like always.

"Hidy, Miz Moore," I said, plopping myself down beside her and clutching the box of blueing close to me. "How's ya garden?"

"Growing good, and how's yourn?"

"Growing good, too."

"Who is that, Nellie?" Mr. Moore called from inside the house.

"Just Olivia Shortt's girl, the runty one."

Feeling like it was her duty to tell me stuff, Mrs. Moore started broadcasting.

She started off by telling me Lou Jean Purvis was in trouble, but I didn't pay any attention because I was watching the horses and figuring how I could get past them without getting killed. Then she told me about the car wreck in front of Henry Moore's— no relation—store.

"Brains all over the road," she said.

Mr. Moore came out. "Let's go, woman."

"We're going to Coaltown now," Mrs. Moore said to me. "Tell your mama 'Hidy' for me."

"Okay," I said, picking myself up with shaking knees to advance to my doom. The Moores' DeSoto rolled down the road in the opposite direction from where I was going. The horses were tickled to death. They fanned out, one on each bank and one in front of me. I was coming upon that one in the road when he raised his head and looked at me.

"I got you now," he said and started toward me.

I ran. Like a rat I ran down the creek bank through the briars and weeds. All of a sudden my feet got tangled up in what was left of an old rusty fence. The blueing sailed into the creek. A broken fence post jumped up and socked me in the mouth. I bounced against it and back onto my feet again without even stopping. I glanced over my shoulder, scared to death. Then I stopped and looked again. The one horse was eating the blueing box in the creek; the other two were still chomping grass on the bank. Blood gushed from my mouth. I squalled.

The horses planned all of it. They knew that old

busted fence was down there, and without even touching me, they had maimed me. Now I was bleeding to death. Mama heard me coming before I rounded the bend and she ran to meet me.

That evening Mama flagged down Josh Clancy and gave him the devil. After that, the horses disappeared. We never saw them again.

That's exactly how I got a lump on my lip. It always reminds me of that lumpy-faced traveling salesman, and of horses. I never read *National Velvet* or *Black Beauty*, and I vowed that when I was married to Roy Rogers, Trigger would have to go.

13

One day, when my lip was nearly healed, me and Junie walked down to Copperhead Bridge. When we got to the bridge we saw and heard Nit coming up the road singing "Barbry Allen" as loud as he could. We ran to meet him.

> *They grew and grew to the mountaintop*
> *And there they grew no higher*
> *And there they tied in a true lover's knot*
> *The rose grew round the briar.*

"Hey, there's my girls!" Nit hollered. "Skinny Ginny and June Moon! Candy for the girls." He dug into his pockets, and Hershey's Kisses rolled all over the road. Me and Junie scrambled for them, giggling.

He was dressed in his denim overalls, a T-shirt, and old worn-out work boots like always. His blond hair was all wet and sticking to his neck and face from his recent shower at the bathhouse. A ring of coal dust circled his glazed blue eyes, and a three-day stubble of beard made his face blue-black.

"Guess who Nit seen not thirty minutes ago, girls?" he said as we walked back toward Copperhead Bridge.

We knew but we said, "Who?"

"Your grandpappy! Old Poppy Shortt!"

"Oh, did you? What'd he say? When's he coming to see us?"

"Soon, soon, he said. He asked after you. 'How's the girls?' he said. 'How's my pretty Skinny Ginny and my pretty June Moon?' says he."

Me and Junie giggled. We knew Poppy didn't say that.

Nit sat down on the narrow bridge railing and took a swig of whiskey. He coughed and grinned. "Well," he said. "I finally have set the date—the very day and hour!"

"What date, Nit?" Junie said. "What are you talking about?"

"The big day I will quit this evil habit of drink.

July 30th at twelve noon. That is the day and hour I will stop my drunken ways. I will never touch another drop!"

"Oh, Nit!" Junie laughed. "You're always saying you're gonna quit. You were supposed to quit last Saturday, remember? But here you are, drunk again."

"Ah, but trouble came, girl. A pain hit me just under my left shoulder blade." Nit strained to reach the spot with his left hand, and teetered dangerously on the narrow railing. Me and Junie steadied him. "When a man is in pain, a little drink is what he needs. Just a little drink."

"Oh, Nit." Junie laughed again. "Face it! You'll never quit drinking, never!"

Nit's face fell, and all of a sudden he looked real old. "You think not, June Moon?" He said it sadly, and I felt sorry for him. "You think me doomed, girl?"

"Well, no, not doomed, Nit. 'Course not! It just so happens I like you when you're drunk," Junie said sweetly.

"You do?"

"Yeah, you're funny and I like you."

"I like you, too," I said.

"But I don't seem to like myself, girls. There's the devil of it. It's important for a man to like hisself."

Forgetting where he was, Nit all of a sudden started to lean backward. Me and Junie squealed and grabbed him. For a moment it seemed like he was bound to fall the eight or ten feet into the creek, but we hauled him up steady again. His beloved bottle, however, slipped out of his pocket and fell into the water below.

"Git it! Git it!" Nit hollered in a panic.

The bottle bobbed in the sun, then disappeared in the shadows under the bridge. We all three scrambled to the other side of the bridge, and half ran, half fell down the creek bank. Big old naked roots stuck out of the washed-out bank. Crawdads scampered into their holes to get out of our way. The rocks in the creek hurt our bare feet, but the water felt good and cool.

"Spread out!" Nit hollered. "Git to the sides, girls! Don't let it past!"

Junie stood on one side of the creek, I stood on the other, and Nit stood in the middle, waiting and watching for the bottle. Nit was bent over, his overalls wet to the knees, his eyes frantic, his hands cupped in the shape of the bottle, ready to grab.

But the bottle didn't come. We waited some more. No bottle. We creeped under the bridge, and the air got cooler and smelled like wet earth.

"I'll never make it back to the liquor store before it closes." Nit groaned. "Gotta git that bottle!"

"It's lodged somewheres," Junie said.

"Don't let it past, girls, and I'll git you a watermelon big as a worshtub."

We went farther under the bridge, feeling with our feet, trying to adjust our eyes to the dimness.

"Yonder it is!" Junie squealed.

"Where'bouts?"

"Lodged against that rock yonder, right in the middle of the creek. It's about to break loose. Spread out!"

"Where, girl, where?"

My eyes got adjusted and I could see the bottle, too, and jagged rock walls holding up the bridge on both sides, the rotting boards over my head where streaks of sunlight striped my face, and green moldy growths on the wood and rocks. I shivered. Nit was breathing heavy as he reached for the bottle with both hands.

At that moment, a movement slithered across the edge of my vision. It was almost the color of the rocks where it lay curled and half hidden. Its pinpoint black eyes, cold as death, rested on my face, not two feet away from me. Many times I had heard the story of the snake hypnotizing its victim with his evil eyes and tongue. "Charming," the old folks called it. "They can charm the birds right out of their nests and rabbits right out of their holes." And at that moment I was charmed, hypnotized, frozen to my spot.

I was vaguely aware of Junie and Nit laughing and walking away.

"C'mon, Ginny."

"What're you looking at, young 'un?"

Just above that snake, another one curled slow among the crevices in the rock wall. The spell broke.

"God a'mighty!" I heard Nit behind me just as a scream found its way out of the bottom of my belly. At the same time I felt Nit's arm grab me about the middle and swing me away from danger. The copperhead struck. I saw its body sail through the air; I heard a dull clunk. Then Nit was hauling me toward the sun. He pushed me up the bank, both of us sobbing. Junie and me pulled him up, and we all three sat down in the road, crying and panting, and trembling.

"It got you, didn't it, Nit?" I wailed. "I heard it hit you."

"No, Ginny, no," Nit said, and smiled a trembly little smile. "No, it never."

His funny smile turned into a grin, then an outright laugh. He laughed and laughed so hard the tears ran down his face all over again, and he rolled over in the road, holding his belly. He wiped his nose on his shirttail.

"The old bottle saved me for once," he managed to say between his spasms of giggling.

"Here!" he patted the lump in his back pocket. "Here's where the old reptile struck me. Bet that bottle broke ever tooth in his head!"

14

Me and Junie were damming up the creek behind our house for a swimming hole the next day. It took us a good hour to build the dam, but it was the best swimming hole we ever made. The water came up to my thighs. Mama was sitting on the back porch, watching us. She was upset about the snakes under the bridge. The night before, some of the men in the holler, along with Nit, had cleaned out the nest of copperheads under the bridge.

"We got six of the rascals, Miz Shortt," they said to Mama. "Don't think there's no more, but you and your girls be careful just the same, you heah?"

"Thank you," Mama said.

She wouldn't let us out of her sight after that.

Tildy came wading down the creek from her house. She had grown up to be twice my size, and she had got so she buttered up the teachers at school and gossiped like old Mrs. Moore. It was getting so I couldn't stand her no more.

"Hidy, June Marie," she called. "Hidy, Ginny."

"Hidy. Come help build our swimming hole," Junie said.

"Mustn't get my dress wet," she said. "See? It's new."

"Mustn't get my dress wet," I mimicked Tildy under my breath.

"Well, your feet's all wet now," I said aloud. "Wonder you don't melt."

That made her mad.

"How's your lip, Virginia Carol?" she said sweetly, knowing I hated to be called Virginia. "It looks real funny."

"My name's Ginny, and my lip don't look as funny as you do!"

Tildy came and stood on the bank beside the swimming hole.

"Folks are all talking about you nearly getting snake-bit, Virginia Carol," she said.

She was just trying to get my goat. I shrugged and piled a glob of mud on the top of our dam.

"What's to talk about?"

"Well, folks are all wondering why old Nit had you and Junie down under the bridge in the first place."

Junie's head shot toward Tildy.

"I said a dozen times we went for his bottle. He dropped it in the creek," I explained.

"Yeah, that's what you said. Folks still wonder, though."

"What're you getting at, Tildy?" Junie said. "Spit it out or swaller it."

Tildy rolled her eyes up to the sky, and smiled. "I promised to zip my lip," she said and pulled an imaginary zipper across her mouth.

Then Junie waded out of the water real slow, eyeing Tildy. "Well, you better tell me what you're talking about, Hilda Matilda Ratliff," she said. "Or I'll duck you, new dress and all, right 'cheer in this swimming hole."

Junie would do it, too.

"Don't get so huffy. You know how folks talk. You three females living alone, with no man to take care of you."

"You better tell me right now," Junie said in a horrible voice.

Tildy looked sick all of a sudden. "Why, you know I don't believe all that stuff, Junie."

"What stuff?"

Tildy was nervous. "Why, you *know* I don't. Me and Ginny's best friends, ain't we, Ginny?"

"What *stuff*, Tildy?" Junie hollered.

"Well, th-they say old N-Nit ain't quite right, that's all."

Tildy began to edge away from Junie.

Junie stepped closer to her, her eyes like blue fire.

Tildy began to shake, and talked real fast. "They say he likes little girls in an unnatural way. They say Nit gives you and Ginny candy and takes advantage of you!"

With these words Tildy turned and started to run back up the creek, but Junie was too quick for her. In a flash, she had Tildy on her face in the creek, fighting for air.

"June Marie Shortt!" Mama called from the porch. "Let her go! I'll whip you good!"

"Who-said-it? Who-said-it?" Junie said over and over, her face red with rage. She knotted her fingers into Tildy's hair, pushed her face into the creek, then let it up again, all in rhythm to her words.

"Miz Mmm . . ." Tildy gurgled on one of her trips up. "Miz Mmmmm . . ."

"Miz Moore?"

Mama reached us then, snatched Junie up by the arm, gave her a swat that sent her staggering, and reached to help Tildy. But Tildy was already halfway home. She scrambled up the creek like one of those old crawdads, squalling all the way.

Mama was nearly as upset as Junie. Her shoes were wet and she stepped out of the creek.

"What in the world got into you, June Marie?" she said, out of breath. "Why'd you treat that child like that?"

"She's an old devil!"

"Don't you talk like that!"

Junie started to cry. Mama looked confused. She didn't know what to say or do. I was enjoying myself.

"She said awful things, Mama," I interjected.

"Who did? Tildy?"

Junie rushed into the house. Me and Mama started walking slow after her.

"Well, what'd she say?"

I watched Mama's face go from red to white as I told her what Tildy said. When I finished, she didn't say a word. We went in the kitchen and Mama took off her wet shoes and set them on the warm end of the cookstove. Still, she didn't say anything. We could hear Junie in the back room crying.

"Ain't it awful, Mama?" I said, fishing for a response from her.

"You mean, 'Isn't it awful?'" she corrected my English and said no more.

"Well, *isn't* it awful what Tildy said?" I hollered, disgusted.

"Saying a thing doesn't make it so," she said.

She sat down at the kitchen table, looking tired and sad.

Then it came to me. In Sweet Creek Holler, saying a thing almost did make it so. It might as well be so, because everybody would believe it anyway. Already the story about us and Nit under the bridge would be making the rounds from tongue to tongue.

"Gather some cucumbers from the garden, Ginny, will you?"

"Is that all you got to say?" I was mad as the devil at her. How come she couldn't get mad and pitch a fit once in a while like other mothers did?

Then my mama, who knew everything, said to me, real serious, "Let me tell you something, Gin-Gin. When you hurt your lip, it wasn't the horses that hurt you, now, was it? No, it was your *fear* of the horses that made you run, and you hurt yourself. Don't you see, it's the same here? These people can't hurt you as long as you are not afraid of them. They can't touch you. Just go on holding your head up high, and remember, you have done nothing wrong."

It was the longest speech I had ever heard from Mama, and I was impressed. I nodded.

"Just don't say a word about this, Gin," she cautioned me. "Anything you say will only fan the flames."

I went out to gather cucumbers.

Supper was not a joyful affair. About everything on our table came fresh from the garden—roastin' ears, green beans and taters, crispy cucumbers and juicy red tomatoes. Then there were the old stand-bys—corn bread and side meat. But it seemed nobody could eat.

"As long as you know it's a lie, and poor Nit knows it's a lie, that's all that counts," Mama said. "Defend yourself if folks mention it to you—but they won't have the guts to say anything to your face. Otherwise, say no more about it."

I talked Junie into going out into the cool night to catch lightnin' bugs with me, her troubles temporarily forgotten. Dora Faye came walking up the road with her little sister, Trula. We just loved Trula. She looked like a doll, and she was the only girl we knew who had only one name.

"Hey, Dora Faye," I called. "Where ya goin' to?"

"Hey, Ginny Carol! Where you been hiding, girl?" she called cheerfully.

Me and Junie started swinging on the gate as Dora Faye and Trula stopped to talk.

"I'm out inviting folks to my wienie roast," Dora Faye said. "Y'all come."

"A wienie roast! When?"

"Tomorrow night, seven-thirty. Y'all do come. Can you bring some candy?"

"Sure," I said.

"Sounds like fun," Junie said. "Who all's coming?"

"Just about everybody in the holler. Lots of girls. Boys, too!"

Junie and Dora Faye giggled, and I groaned. Except for Junior Longridge, I still hated every boy in the world. And all parties these days seemed to turn into kissing parties.

Me and Junie went into the bedroom and looked

over our shorts. Junie would wear her navy ones with a blue shirt Mama made her, and I would wear my red shorts with the cotton cherry blouse Cousin Lucy Lee sent me from Roanoke. It was white with red rickrack trim and little sprigs of plastic cherries at the neck.

"We're going to a wienie roast!" we said to Mama. "We're going to make some fudge to take!"

But Mama didn't hear a word we said. She was sitting with an open book on her lap and looking out at the clouds as if she saw another world there. She was in one of her moods.

15

The next day, while Mama worked in the garden, me and Junie set about making peanut-butter fudge. Before long, we had all the makin's bubbling away in a skillet on top of the cookstove.

"I wisht I had a new hairdo," Junie said. "I seen a pitcher of Debbie Reynolds in one of your movie magazines, and she had her hair all wound around in a knot on top of her head. It looked real pretty."

"Then why don't you fix yours like that?"

"It ain't long enough. I wisht I had some old

catalogues, but you done cut 'em all up for paper dolls. I can always find some fancy do in a catalogue."

"Yeah, I wisht we had some old catalogues, too."

"I bet Miz Clancy's got some old catalogues," Junie said.

"What?"

"Nobody ever asks Miz Clancy for old catalogues. I bet she's got loads of 'em. I think you orta go ask her."

I looked at Junie with disbelief. Ask Mrs. Clancy for old catalogues?

"*You* ask her!" I said.

"Huh! You're the one that'll cut 'em up for paper dolls. I'm too old for paper dolls."

"But it's you wants to look at hairdos."

"When I get through looking at hairdos, then they're all yours. So who wants 'em more?"

"I'm not going," I said weakly.

"You mean you're not going to tell Mama," she said, and she poured the candy into a clean white dish. "No, we won't tell Mama."

I followed her out the door without thinking a lot about what might actually happen to us if we went up and knocked on Mrs. Clancy's front door. No child ever had done that in the history of the world. Now, some grown folks might have done it once in a while, but never a child. Nobody ever went into the Clancy house except Josh. Sometimes, if you got up real early on a warm morning, you might just barely see the old witch's bonnet tipping around the side of the house where she worked on her flowers. But if you got anywhere near her, she went back inside. She was real old, maybe fifty, and she didn't like children or neighbors, or fresh air, or canning vegetables like the other women of Sweet Creek Holler. And nobody ever remembered hearing her say more than a few words at a time except once when Bubba Ratliff put a rock through her living-room window. She said plenty that day, but Bubba didn't stay around long enough to hear it all.

The housewives, naturally, talked about her. They said she was highfalutin and proud, and nastier things. But us kids, we were just scared of her and the Clancy house.

"What'll you say?" I said to Junie, feeling my knees knock together.

"You mean, what'll *you* say," Junie said. "I'm just going along."

"Well, I don't know what to say."

"What're you going for?"

"The catalogues."

"Then just say that."

"Maybe Josh will be there. I ain't skeered of him much."

"No, the truck's gone. Josh ain't home."

We tippy-toed across the Clancy yard like it was a wooden floor with creaky boards. Then we stopped and stared at the front door.

"Go on, Ginny," Junie nudged me. "Knock."

I walked up the steps, gulped, and knocked lightly. "Nobody home," I said quickly. "Let's go."

"You know she's home. She's always home. Knock louder."

I knocked again, louder.

The door opened before I was even finished knocking, and there stood the black-eyed, black-headed Clancy witch frowning down at me. I backed down the steps. I forgot what I was supposed to say.

"Ask her!" Junie gouged me.

"You got any . . . ?" I faltered and failed.

Mrs. Clancy frowned deeper and started to close the door.

"You got any old catalogues, Miz Clancy?" Junie said, her voice not even shaking. "Ginny likes to cut 'em up for paper dolls."

I looked at Junie with growing respect.

Mrs. Clancy peeped out at us for a good long while. Then she made a gesture toward the right corner of the house.

"In the cellar," she said in this tiny voice. "Take all you want."

Then she closed the door.

"In the cellar." Junie laughed, her eyes bright with excitement.

We headed around the right corner of the house where the rickety old cellar steps led down under the house. Nobody else we knew had a cellar. Junie trooped down the steps without a thought, but I hung back.

"I ain't going down there," I said. "It's hard telling what's down there. We might never come up again."

Junie hesitated on the steps and looked back at me, seeming worried for about a second.

"Junie," I said, "maybe you don't remember how scary the ghosts are. You saw them just one time and that was five years ago! Maybe they are waiting for us in the cellar. Maybe they live down there!"

Junie looked at the big wooden door in front of her, then laughed and tossed her head like she was tossing away her fears.

"Ghosts don't *live* anywhere. They're dead! Now come on, fraidy-cat!" she said and turned the door knob.

The cellar door swung open. I saw my sister disappear into the cellar, and I glanced around me, not knowing what to do. I thought I saw the curtain move at the window above the cellar, so I hightailed it down the steps after June Marie.

There was no light in the cellar, but there were plenty of windows at ground level, so that we could see a little. We were in one big room that smelled like mold. A whole bunch of shelves lined the walls. They were filled with stuff like store-bought canned food, carpenter's tools, old musty books, old rusty mining junk, old dusty boxes, and catalogues! We fell on them—Sears Roebuck, Montgomery Ward, Spiegel, Aldens—the works. Worlds and worlds of old catalogues. We crammed our arms full and left real quick. We ran down the road all loaded down and laughing up a storm. At home we dumped the catalogues on the porch and poured over them.

"They're moldy outside and round the edges," Junie said. "But they look pretty good inside."

"1929!" I hollered. "This is a 1929 catalogue, Junie! Look at these dresses!"

"Mine's 1938!" Junie squealed. "1938, Ginny!"

Junie started flipping through that catalogue like she was looking for something special.

Old Buddy, the best dog in Virginia, came up on the porch and wagged his tail at me. I put my arms around him and kissed his sweet face. He sure enough was a lovable old thing.

"Look, Ginny," Junie said real low, a funny expression on her face. "Look at this."

I looked at what she pointed to in the 1938 catalogue. In red crayon, somebody had circled a little girl's white sailor dress.

16

It looked like Dora Faye's wienie roast was going to be the best party ever. Mama walked us down the road to where the Mayfields lived, and said she'd come back for us at eleven. We were not to leave until she came for us. I guess she still had snakes on her mind.

There was a flat clearing in the woods behind the Mayfield house where they already had a big fire going from old tires. They stunk to high heaven.

We handed our plate of candy to Mrs. Mayfield, then joined the other children squatting Indian-fashion on the ground around the fire. Clevis Ratliff was there with his fiddle, and Susie Ruth had her Jew's harp. Junior wasn't there, which was fine with me. Any time I found myself in his presence seemed like I turned into a pure-tee fool. Me and Junie sat there for a while, our eyes bugging out, watching folks; then Dora Faye, giggling, said we would play Drop the Clothespin, and me and Junie joined in.

Drop the Clothespin was always easy for me because I was short and closer to the bottle than anyone else. You had to stand on one foot, away from the bottle, hold the pins straight out in front of you, aim the pins into the skinny neck of a milk bottle, and drop. The object was to get as many pins as possible inside the bottle. The winner got a prize—usually a Pepsi-Cola.

I was aiming real good when the group all of a sudden got quiet and I thought everybody was looking at me. It made me nervous and I missed. But when I glanced up, nobody was looking at me a'tall. They were all looking at somebody who had walked up behind me quiet as snow. It was Lou Jean, standing there with her arms folded across her middle, seeming uneasy. She looked like a little girl, and her light hair was kinda stringy; it wasn't like Lou Jean to let herself go. She stayed where she was, staring at the ground.

"Hey, Lou Jean," I said, cheerful as could be. "You wanna be next?"

"Hey, Ginny," she said in a whisper. "No, you go on and play. You're doing real good."

Something was wrong and I didn't know what. It had to do with Lou Jean standing there with her arms folded and looking sick. Clevis Ratliff took his turn at the bottle and everybody began to talk all at the same time. I noticed Lou Jean squatting outside the circle a little ways and still not looking at anybody.

Junie darted past me and I grabbed her.

"What's wrong?" I whispered to her. "Why's everybody acting so funny?"

"Hush up!" Junie said, and brushed me off.

I went over and sat down beside Lou Jean. "Hey, Lou Jean," I said to her.

She turned and smiled just a little, like she really didn't see me. Then she started staring into the fire.

Suddenly it came to me. The day I was sitting on Mrs. Moore's porch worrying about the horses, she had told me that Lou Jean was in trouble. In Sweet Creek Holler "in trouble" had only one meaning: Lou Jean was going to have a baby, and her beau, Will Jenkins, was gone to the army. That explained a lot of things. Lou Jean's tummy was showing a lump, and that's why she kept her arms folded there. And that was why she was acting so funny, along with everybody else. And her mother—yes! That's why her mother acted like she wanted to trade her off to a stranger!

Pretty soon the play turned to kissing games. I was as old as some of the others, but I didn't see anything so interesting about kissing boys. I guess I didn't interest them either 'cause nobody asked me to play Post Office. A few other boys and girls my age or younger just sat and watched, but everybody else participated, except Lou Jean. She kept glancing over her shoulder like she wanted to leave but was afraid to because folks would all stare at her again.

I wondered why she would come to a party when

she must know everybody was talking about her. Then I knew, and a great rush of pity went through me. She wanted to be accepted. She wanted to know we were still her friends, and nobody was paying her any attention at all. I was trying to think of something to say to her when Dora Faye came up beside me and whispered, "Will you toast these marshmellers for me, Ginny?"

"Sure," I said, taking the stick from her hand.

About six marshmallows were speared on the stick, which I put in the fire. I glanced over at Lou Jean, wanting to comfort her, but I didn't know how. She was unaware that I was there, as the flames curled into blue images before us. I was hypnotized into a dreamlike state as the images in the fire became clear, and suddenly the night was frosty, crisp, a long-ago winter darkness. The clearing was gone, the other children gone, and in their place two little yella-headed girls, wrapped in red blankets, were huddled around another fire in another part of the woods.

"She's the prettiest little baby I ever did see," the larger girl was saying. "I wish she was my little sister. Did you see her dimples?"

"But I'm your little sister, Lenora! Don't you like me anymore?"

"Of course I do! You'll always be my little sister, no matter what. And my best friend, too!"

The girls hugged each other in the coldness.

"Her name is Lou Jean," the little girl said. "Such a pretty name for a pretty baby. We'll have babies someday, won't we, Lenora?"

Lenora's face clouded. "I don't know, Shirley."

"Ginny Carol!" Dora Faye was hollering at me, and I came back to the present with a gasp. The oppressive summer heat hit me.

"You've burned them all to a crisp!" Dora Faye said irritably, taking the marshmallows from my trembling hand. "What's the matter with you? You look like you've seen a ghost!"

I couldn't speak, and Dora Faye stood there glaring at me, with her hands on her hips. I looked at Lou Jean, but she was still gazing into the flames as if she, too, saw something there.

"To heck with it!" Dora Faye said, tossing all the marshmallows into the flames and bouncing away.

The other children were gathering around the fire again, laughing and toasting wienies. Then the grownups started drifting in to eat and drink and tell stories.

Suddenly someone appeared out of the darkness and stomped into the firelight. She was seven feet tall. "Lou Jean Purvis!" she hollered, as her eyes fell on the girl.

Lou Jean seemed to shrivel up right before our

eyes. She looked for all the world like a little old woman, her eyes taking up most of her face.

"Yes, Ma."

"Git your sinful self up and come home with me, girl."

"Yes, Ma."

Lou Jean stood up, trembling, and walked to her mother.

"Ain't you got no shame, girl? Ain't you done enough without parading your sins in public?"

The big woman burned her daughter to nakedness. Lou Jean didn't answer. Her shame was eating at her like acid, but she didn't cry. She just stood there looking at the ground. Then mother and daughter disappeared into the night.

Mama came at eleven just like she promised, and it was good to see her face, pure and sweet. We walked home in silence. Mama was moody, and me and Junie were still trying to sort out impressions from the scenes behind us. We could hear the whippoorwill as clear and perfect as a voice in the night saying, "Whip-poor-Will."

"Poor Will. Poor Will," I chanted.

"Poor Lou Jean," Junie whispered. "Poor, poor Lou Jean."

The moon was full, and night shadows fell across the road, slicing us in half sometimes. Before we reached the bridge, Mama picked up a big rock in case we saw a snake, and she told me and Junie to walk close to her in the middle of the road, and keep our eyes wide open. But the snakes did not rear their copper heads that night, at least not in our world, where Mama kept us safe.

17

All the next day I worried about Lou Jean, but Mama didn't want me to go up to her house. Seemed like Mama was obsessed with snakes. Not only that, but the gossip worried her, too. The only thing she would say was, "Lou Jean doesn't want to be bothered with you right now."

Finally, though, after I begged her ragged, she said, "Okay, you can go, but Junie has to go with you."

Junie didn't want to go, but she did, just so I would shut up. When we got there, we found Lou Jean and her daddy sitting on the front-porch swing.

"Hidy, girls." Nit grinned. He was drinking, but he wasn't drunk yet. "How ya doin'?"

"Hidy, Nit, Lou Jean," we said and sat down on the porch steps.

Lou Jean smiled at us. She seemed at ease. I soon

found out why. Her mama was gone to a wake up on Bishop Ridge and wouldn't be home till tomorrow. I relaxed. We sat and talked awhile, then Junie started nudging me to go home. I wanted to talk to Lou Jean and listen to her laughing a bit, and make sure she was going to be all right.

"What you whispering about?" Nit wanted to know.

"Junie wants to go home, and I want to stay," I said.

"Then let her go home and you stay."

"Mama wants Junie with me all the time," I said, disgusted. "Or somebody or other with me. She reckons the snakes won't get me if Junie's with me. She worries about snakes all the time now."

Nit laughed. "Don't much blame her. Them's nasty boogers. But you, Junie Marooney, you go on home before it gets dark, and tell your mama that I'll see Miss Ginny Penny home whenever she wants to go. I'll walk her down the road to make sure the snakes don't git her. Didn't I see about her last time?"

"You don't mind, Nit?"

"Not a speck. You go on."

That meant I could stay as long as I wanted, and I was tickled. Nit started telling us a story about old Rawhide and Bloody Bones, and I moved up closer to him and Lou Jean to sit on a chair.

When he got to the *"I gotcha!"* part, I about jumped out of my hide, and Lou Jean giggled. I was feeling good. It looked like Lou Jean was all right. It was getting dark and everything got quiet.

Then out of the clear blue Nit spoke. "Did you burn the Clancy barn, child?" he asked Lou Jean.

"No, Pa. I never."

"Your ma says you's down that way and you had matches in your pocket."

"I didn't burn the barn, though."

"Then where were you, Lou Jean, girl?"

"Down to the spring house, cooling my feet."

Nit slipped the bottle of whiskey out of his back pocket and took a swig. "Did your mama pick on you that day?"

"No more'n usual."

"Did anything out of the ordinary happen?"

"Just a man come by selling encyclopedias."

"Did you want to buy 'em?"

"Not 'specially . . . Ginny was here." Lou Jean eyed me. I knew she didn't want to tell on her mama for trying to sell her off. I wouldn't tell that.

Lou Jean turned her face toward the moon and moved her lips silently. "What'd you do that fer?" Nit said.

"What?"

"Talking to yourself. You's saying something."

She stared at her father in surprise. "Did I? Did I say any words?"

"Not out loud."

"Then what, then?"

"You moved your mouth like you's talking to the moon."

Lou Jean dropped her head.

I shuffled around, feeling uneasy.

"I didn't say nothing, Pa."

"Where's Will lately, Lou? Why ain't Will been around?"

"Don't talk about Will."

"You and Will bust up? That's why you mope around and talk to the moon?"

"Don't talk about Will."

"That's why you burned the barn?"

"I never burned no barn."

"You been known to set fires before, girl." His voice was just a whisper.

Her head jerked up and she looked from him to me and back again.

"What fires? When? I hate fire! I do. It scares me most to death, more'n anything. Why would I set a fire?" Her voice quavered out of control. "Why would I do that, Pa? Tell me why . . . ?"

"I dunno, child. I just don't know."

"Look at the moon, Pa!" she said with nervous

excitement in her voice, and laughed. " 'Member when I was just a little girl you used to walk me down the road a piece in the moonlight?"

"Lou . . ."

"Walk me now, Pa. Come on." She stood up quickly and jumped off the porch.

"Let's wait till Ginny's ready to go home," he said.

"I'm ready now," I said.

Nit and me jumped off the porch.

"I won't tell on you," Nit said and took Lou Jean's hand. "And Ginny knows how to keep a secret, don't you, Ginny Penny?"

"I won't tell."

"But I swear to God, Lou my lass, if you don't quit playing with fire, I'll be bound to do something."

"Lookee at the lightnin' bugs!" she squealed. "Reckon the fire burns their tails, Pa? Reckon it hurts?"

"I reckon not."

We walked down the hill to the road, slow.

"I don't like fire," Lou Jean said again. "I don't want to burn in hell."

She started breathing fast and uneven.

"Burn in hell!" Nit let go of her hand and stared at her small white face in the moonlight. "S'that what worries you?"

"Ma says I'll burn in hell."

"Ma's crazy. Pay her no mind."

"Oh, no, she's right, Pa. You've been drunk for months now. You don't know what's happened right under your nose. I've been so bad."

"What don't I know?"

"Ma's gonna tell you, but she dreads telling you 'cause she says you'll go on the biggest binge ever and miss work. I begged her to let me tell you."

"Tell me what, child?"

"Pa, I wisht you didn't drink so much."

"What's the matter, Lou Jean?"

"I'm going to have a baby. Soon as Will found out, he took off for the army. Mama says everybody in the holler knows—Ginny knows—just a little girl and she knows. Everybody knows 'cept you! And you'd know, too, if you'd been sober long enough to listen and see. Mama says everybody's laughing at her behind her back. She says I done it on purpose to spite her. Pa, what am I going to do?"

Throughout this breathless speech, Nit stood flabbergasted in the middle of the road, staring at her. "A baby?" he croaked.

"Yeah, Pa. A baby. Due in November, I figger. And Ma's gone crazy with shame. Why, I can't tell you the awful thing she done . . ."

"But you're just a little girl," he interrupted.

"I'm sixteen, Pa," she said. "I wisht I was a little girl again. Littler than Ginny, here . . . littler than anybody."

"A baby? Oh, Lou . . ." His voice broke, and he put one arm around her. "What's your ma put you through? How long has she knowed?"

"I told her on the last day of school."

"Lordy, did she know the day you burned the barn?"

"I never burned no barn," she said real quick.

Their eyes held until she looked away and studied the moon. "I never," she repeated.

"Don't matter now." He sighed. "I'll try . . . I'll do my best to protect you, Lou. I swear, girl, I'll try . . . but your mama . . . she's crazy . . ." His voice trailed off.

"You could quit drinking, Pa. Ma's always in a better mood when you don't drink so much."

"All right, I swear . . . I swear on my first grandbaby here." Real soft, he placed his hand on her swollen belly. "I swear."

Lou Jean smiled. "You make it seem not so bad," she said. "Like maybe it won't be awful to have a grandbaby."

"It won't be awful," he mumbled and put his arm around her again.

We started walking down the road, quiet. Nit was running his free hand nervously through his hair;

Lou Jean was hugging herself like she was cold. And I was thinking how our Lou Jean was sorely troubled in spirit.

The summer sounds were all around us—the crickets, the frogs. The valley deepened between the hills, crawling from the moon, and dark shadows fell across the road.

"Who's there?" It was the voice of Dora Faye as she stopped in the road. She was holding on to her little sister's hand, watching us approach her.

"Lou Jean Purvis," Lou Jean said. "And my pa and Ginny Carol."

"Oh." Dora Faye giggled nervously. "I declare, you gave me a fright."

We stood in the dark, just able to see each other's faces in the moonlight. Lou Jean, seeming embarrassed with her pa's arm around her, shrugged away from him.

"What you doing all the way up here in the dark?" Nit said. "Ain't you afraid the boogers'll git you?"

"They're more skeered of me than I am of them." Dora Faye giggled again. "I'm just on my way to see Miz Purvis on account of my mama wants her recipe for pickled corn. She sent me out in this dark to get a recipe. You ever heard the beat?"

"Ma ain't home," Lou Jean said. "I'll bring you the recipe tomorrow, though."

"We'll find it when we git through walking Ginny

home," Nit said, "and I'll bring it by on my way to work, all right?"

"Reckon so."

"You come on now and let us walk you home, too."

"All right."

We all walked down the road together.

"I'm wore out," Trula said suddenly, and we all couldn't help laughing.

"Wore out, huh?" Nit laughed as he swung the child easily to his shoulder. "Well, how's that?"

Trula giggled.

"I don't reckon she needs to be carried," Dora Faye stammered all of a sudden. "She's too old to be carried on a man's shoulder."

"Didn't you hear the lamb? She's wore out," Nit said and patted the little girl's bare leg.

"Ma wouldn't like it," Dora Faye said.

Nit and Lou Jean looked at her funny.

"Well . . ." Dora Faye said, real nervous. "Well, you know how my ma is."

Nobody else spoke.

"You know my ma."

The night breeze cooled our cheeks. The creek rippled over the rocks in the dark, and the unanswered questions lay still in secret thoughts. Nit and Lou Jean didn't understand, but I did. I knew why

Dora Faye didn't want Nit holding little Trula on his shoulder. And it made my heart hurt.

18

Revival at the Church of Jesus was losing its appeal to us because just about everybody in the holler had been saved at one time or another. I had managed to resist the urge to rush up to the altar myself, and Junie never did get the urge. Sometimes people looked at us woefully, like they were praying for our poor lost souls, but Mama would say, "No need to make a spectacle of yourselves."

But the rest of the holler was about ninety-nine and forty-four-hundredths percent pure. Junie and me decided to go to the revival on the first night because Little Brother Arkansas was returning to preach. He was now twenty-one years old, but he still put you in mind of a pretty little boy.

"Just as I am / Without one plea / But that Thy blood / Was shed for me . . ." The old hymn was wailed over and over, while Little Brother stood up there crying and pleading for the sinners to come to Jesus. I was just about to go to sleep when Junie gouged me. I looked up and there was Lou Jean going up the aisle, looking small and scared. Her face was white as death and she kept her arms folded across her middle. There was not a single sound in that tiny church. Lou Jean knelt before the Arkansas Christ Child, and he put his hand on her head, saying, "God bless you, sister. What is your name?"

A sob came up when she told him her name.

"Repeat after me, sister," Little Brother said. "I, Lou Jean Purvis . . ."

Lou Jean's voice trembled as she repeated the well-known phrases. "I don't want to go to hell," she said then. "Save me from hell, Little Brother."

On the way home, Mrs. Moore and two of her ugly freckled-faced young 'uns sat in the front seat of the church bus. Me and Junie sat behind them. Lou Jean had caught a ride with somebody. Mrs. Moore was hollering across the aisle to Mrs. Looney about the revival. Then they put their heads together in the aisle and I could hear some of their whispers.

"That Lou Jean . . . loose girl . . . sympathy . . . after Little Brother . . . crazy Mama . . ."

Me and Junie were quiet, listening, and I could feel Junie tensing up like she was getting mad. We glanced at each other and I could see the glint in her eye. Since the day of her fight with Tildy, we hadn't mentioned the gossip about us and Nit, or Mrs. Moore's role in spreading it.

"Don't fan the flames," Mama had told us, and we had done as she said. We hadn't seen poor Nit lately, for he had taken to riding to and from work with Claude Estep in his pickup. Mrs. Moore's voice dropped and me and Junie froze when we heard: "Nit and Olivia's girls."

"Heard all about it," Mrs. Looney said.

"Shh . . ." from Mrs. Moore. "Bzz . . . buzz . . . snake . . . bridge."

With that, Junie flew to her feet and charged between the two women, leaning into the aisle.

"I hate people who go to church, then spread lies about their neighbors!" she yelled.

Everybody shut up and listened.

"What! What are you talking about, girl?" Mrs. Moore said, sounding nervous. You could just barely see her eyes in the dark.

"Lies! All lies!" Junie yelled louder.

"What lies?" Mrs. Moore screeched. "Are you crazy, June Marie Shortt? We were just talking about snakes under y'all's bridge. There *was* snakes, wasn't they?"

"Yeah, and there's snakes on this bus, too!"

"Why, June Marie Shortt, your mama'll hear of this!"

"Leave my mama out of this and mind your own business for a change."

"Well, I'll swaney! I never had a child talk to me so."

"Swaney all you want to, you old gossip. Just quit spreading lies about me and my sister!"

"Sow up front!" the bus driver hollered all of a sudden as the bus came to a stop in the middle of the road.

He was talking about a fat old sow hog that was ambling across the road like she had all night, but all the passengers got the silly giggles 'cause it sounded like he was talking about Mrs. Moore. She was really mad then.

"You'll pay for this," she hissed at us. "You'll pay." And pay we did.

19

Alvie Boxley started hanging around our house all the time. At first I thought it was Mama's blackberry dumplings that kept him coming back. Then I noticed he didn't eat as many blackberry dumplings as he let on, and he was always staring at Junie. Funny thing was, she stared back, and sometimes they smiled this sickening smile at each other that just about turned my stomach.

I would say, "Ugh!" It was the year for "ugh."

The fair came to our county every summer, and

me and Junie usually didn't get to go, because we didn't have a ride. Alvie was sixteen and had his driver's license. It was then I kinda liked old Alvie because he asked Junie to go to the fair with him in his daddy's pickup, and Mama said Junie couldn't go unless she took me along. Realizing that was the only way Junie could go, Alvie agreed to take me, too.

Like all the other girls, me and Junie had crinolines—those starchy mesh petticoats you wore under your dress to make it stand out. The problem with those crinolines was that they lost their stiffness on you and went limp no matter how much you starched them. What you did then was wear two crinolines, then four or six—as many as it took to hold your dress out like an umbrella. It was the style.

For the fair, though, I decided to wear pedal pushers and be free. But Junie, being a young lady of fourteen, wore all her crinolines and mine, too, under her red skirt. She wore her off-the-shoulder gypsy blouse which Mama'd bought her for $1.98 from the Aldens catalogue.

I helped her knot the petticoats around her waist, which leads me to another problem we had with those stupid crinolines. The weight of them stretched the elastic around the middle till you had to knot them up time after time around your waist to keep them from falling off. I guess Junie had on about four or five crinolines all tied up in one big knot on the right side of her waist. Good thing her gypsy blouse was full and fluffy, or she would have looked deformed with that big lump on her side.

In her pretty red skirt and white gypsy blouse, her blue eyes just sparkling and her blond hair all curly and fluffy around her face, Junie looked for all the world like a Christmas-tree ornament.

Alvie arrived about thirty minutes early and sat like a wooden Indian in the living room, waiting for Junie to get dressed. Every time Mama spoke to him, he about jumped out of his hide.

I was feeling kindly toward Alvie and Junie that evening. I forgave the silly way they looked at each other. I had a dollar in change tied up in a handkerchief. At ten cents a ride, I could do eight things and still have enough money for cotton candy, a candy apple, a snow cone, and a bottle of pop.

It took us fifteen minutes to ride down to the fairgrounds on the river. Everybody from a dozen hollers was there because it was kids' night, which meant all children could get in free until seven. The lights were flashing already, even though it wasn't dark for two hours yet. A different tune was playing from every ride, every stall, every freak show, every concession. A barker barked his special show every ten or twelve feet. There was so much to look at, two eyes were not enough.

Alvie wanted to go to the freak-people shows. There wasn't nothing more interesting, he said, than to see two people growed together, or an animal woman who ate snakes. It sounded fascinating to me, too, but Mama had forbidden it.

"No need to laugh at unfortunate people," she had said. "And June Marie Shortt, if you take your sister anywhere near a freak show, I'll fan your tanny!"

Junie told all that to Alvie and he sulked a little, looking at me with fire in his eyes. He was thinking he could talk Junie into going with him if I wasn't along, which was probably true. I gave Alvie a great big smile.

"Okay," Alvie said. "The Ferris wheel, then!"

We headed toward the Ferris wheel. There was a line a mile long, but we paid our ten cents each for tickets and stood with the others waiting. With my eyes all bugged out, trying to take in everything, it took me a while to realize that Alvie and Junie kept whispering together, edging away from me, like they were trying to lose me in the crowd. But once I understood their sneaky moves, I was plenty mad. They sure as the world wouldn't get away from me! I wasn't going to ride the Ferris wheel by myself. I stuck to Junie like flypaper.

Then along came Dora Faye and Tildy, all giggly and squealy, and I almost forgot Alvie and Junie.

When I remembered again, and looked around, there they were, climbing on the Ferris wheel. I made a dash for them, determined not to be left out.

Junie was putting one foot in the car when I grabbed her waist and gave a mighty jerk. "You ain't leaving me to ride alone!"

Junie stood still and half turned to face me. The crowd suddenly roared, and in horror I saw what they were laughing at. All around Junie's feet lay the crinolines in fluffy heaps. I had jerked the knot out of her petticoats.

Not knowing what to do, neither of us moved. Then Junie, her face like a poppy, stepped out of the folded mesh, wrapped it daintily over one arm, and crumbled into the waiting car. Alvie flopped down beside her, and I squeezed in on the other side. The crowd was still laughing and pointing at us when we sailed away.

"I'm awful sorry, Junie," I mumbled when we were high above the fairgrounds.

"I will never speak to you ever again, never, never as long as we both shall live," she choked.

And I shut up.

Alvie huddled, miserable, in one corner, and I huddled, miserable, in the other corner. Junie sank down, like a butterfly with all the stuff rubbed off its wings, the petticoats blowing up in her face.

We didn't hang around the fairgrounds after that.

We went to the pickup without a word, among stares and snickers, and climbed aboard and slunk home.

Once back home, Junie said goodbye to Alvie and we climbed out of the pickup. Then she went into the house and, still without a word, stuffed the petticoats into the cold cookstove and disappeared into the back bedroom. Later Mama dug the petticoats out of the ashes and washed them, but we didn't see hide nor hair of Junie until around noon the next day, which was fine with me, 'cause I couldn't stand the look on her face.

20

I could get so involved in a game of play like with Dora Faye that we would be at it for days. Two weeks after the fair, we were working on a new episode in the abandoned chicken coop in Dora Faye's back yard. We were the starlets Anne and Jeannette right in the middle of dressing up for a big date when Junie hollered up the hill to Dora Faye.

"Dora Faye Mayfield, tell a certain person up there that her mama said for her to come home to supper this instant or she'd know the reason why."

That certain person, of course, was me. Junie was

as good as her word; she hadn't spoken to me since I jerked her petticoats off at the fair. She could be the stubbornest.

I jumped out of the henhouse and headed home. Mama and Junie were at the table when I got there.

"Wash your hands," Mama said coldly, and I did. Then I sat down, ready for a good going-over. It was plain they were both put out with me. We filled up our plates.

Mama said, "Ginny Carol, seems like we have to fetch you for every meal. You want to move in with the Mayfields?"

"You know I don't."

"What in the world do you girls do up there, anyway?"

"Nothin'."

"Nothing? All day?"

"We just play."

"Well, I know Mrs. Mayfield gets tired of you."

"No, she don't. We don't play in the house."

Mama sighed and began to eat. I stuffed my face, thinking she would say no more. I was wrong.

"Well, from now on, you are to stay home and help take care of the house and garden."

"But, Mama . . ."

"But Mama nothing. I may be going to work the first of October."

"Work!" me and Junie said together.

"Yes, work."

Mama had been hoping for a long time that a suitable job for her would become available. Now, she told us, the Sweet Creek Holler postmistress was retiring. The job paid $98 a month and she was going after it.

"I have to take the civil-service test tomorrow," she said.

Me and Junie played with our food. This was a turn of events to think on mightily. We never really expected Mama to get a job. Our mama a working woman? I looked at her then and she was smiling. She was happy. Maybe a job like working in the post office would make her feel important. It *was* an important job. And $98 a month was a lot of money.

"I think that's okay," I said, knowing Mama yearned for our approval.

"We really need the money," she said and looked at Junie.

"Yeah," Junie said. "And we can have more things, can't we?"

"Naturally."

Mama seemed to breathe a sigh of relief. Then we all smiled. Our mama was going to be the new postmistress of Sweet Creek Holler.

After supper, me and old Buddy slipped off again to see Dora Faye.

"Mama's canning tomatoes tomorrow," Dora Faye

said. "And Aunt Gertie Jenkins has got all the rest of our jar lids. So I gotta walk down there and fetch 'em. Come on, go with me."

"All right, but if we ain't back by dark, Mama'll skin me alive. She's already plum put out with me."

"Oh, I reckon we'll be back long before dark," Dora Faye assured me.

So off we went down the road, playing Anne and Jeannette along the way.

Mrs. Moore was sitting on her front porch.

"Hidy, Dora Faye," she hollered, ignoring me.

"Hidy, Miz Moore," Dora Faye answered.

"Hear about the Clancys gittin' a new truck?" Mrs. Moore said.

"No, did they git a new truck?" Dora Faye said.

"Yeah, new Ford. Clancys must have enough money to buy up the holler if they want to. Clancys are real high-class, ain't they?"

"Reckon so."

"Not like some folks I know," Mrs. Moore went on. "Some folks raise up their young 'uns to think they're something special when they ain't nothing but trash."

Me and Dora Faye went on walking, hoping she'd shut up, but she didn't.

"Hear about a certain person taking off her petticoats at the fair?"

I stopped dead in my tracks and looked at Mrs. Moore.

She grinned. "Right in front of everybody, they say," she went on.

"Who said that?" I shouted.

"Well, who pulled your chain, Ginny Carol Shortt?"

"Come on." Dora Faye grabbed my arm. "Pay her no mind."

I started to move on slowly with Dora Faye.

"I bet Olivia Shortt wishes she could buy a new Ford," the old vulture went on.

"We can!" I exploded, not even stopping to consider who I was talking to. "My mama's gonna be the new postmistress of Sweet Creek, and she's gonna make $98 a month. She's taking the test tomorrow."

"Is that a fact, now?" Mrs. Moore said nastily. "Well, la-di-da."

"Yes, that's a fact!" I retorted, tossed my head in the air, and trotted away with Dora Faye. Mrs. Moore was still talking, but we were out of earshot. Then here come Nit Purvis walking up the road.

"Nit!" I cried out and ran to meet him. I felt like hugging him, but I didn't. Mrs. Moore was watching.

"Hello, Ginny, Dora Faye," he said, polite as could be, and I stopped dead in my tracks for the second time, and gave him the eye. He was clean-shaven and neat right down to his eyeballs, where there was no ring of coal dust. He didn't even stagger. He didn't grin, either.

"What's wrong, Nit?" I said.

"Wrong? Nothin's wrong."

He walked way around me, like he was afraid we'd accidentally touch, then went right on walking, like he didn't care to stop and chat. I looked after him, feeling let down.

"Nit . . . ?"

He turned once and glanced back at us. Then he went on.

"He's sober," Dora Faye said.

Yeah, that was it. Nit was sober, and I didn't think I liked him sober a'tall. What good is it having a local drunk if he's gonna go out and sober up on you?

Me and Dora Faye passed about twenty cows on our way to the Jenkinses'. Except for my family, nearly everybody in Sweet Creek Holler had at least one cow; some had two or more. Very few people had barns or pastures for their cows, so they ran free like those sorry Clancy horses had. But cows on the loose made no difference to me because I wasn't afraid of them. They were too stupid to hurt you.

Me and Dora Faye pretended the cows were cars carrying some of Anne and Jeannette's best friends. Like the Moores' old cow—a '53 Guernsey hauling Elizabeth Taylor and Michael Wilding. They waved to us and stopped for a chat. Lana Turner was in a new Jersey, and Rory Calhoun sported a little red heifer.

The Jenkinses were having supper when we went

in, and they invited us to join them; but since both of us already ate, we sat politely in the front room until they were done. It was the height of rudeness in Sweet Creek Holler to sit and watch folks eat, or talk with them or interfere with a meal in any way. So I sat there twisting my dress tail into knots and watching the darkness creep around the windows. Mama was sure enough going to kill me.

Finally Mrs. Jenkins came into the front room to join us. Right off, Dora Faye told her what we were there for, but it was too late for me. It was coal-black outside. We grabbed the poke of jar lids and high-tailed it back up the road. There was no moon and hardly any stars to be seen. The creek was just a black hole on one side of the road, and the mountain was a black hump on the other.

"Tell her it was my fault," Dora Faye tried to comfort me, as we groped along in the dark.

"It won't make no difference," I said in despair. "She'll beat me to a bloody pulp. Let's hurry."

We began to walk faster, but running was risky. It was so dark we couldn't see our hands in front of our faces. We were moving along pretty good when all of a sudden *ker-thump!* I landed flat on my belly atop this big, warm lump of something.

"*Moo-oo!*" the lump bellered out, jerked up, and lifted me about ten feet in the air. My chin clunked her backbone and my bare feet thumped her udders.

I bet I scared that old cow out of a year's supply of milk, but she scared me worse.

"What in thunderation . . . ?" Dora Faye cried out, unable to see what was going on.

"*Horse hockey!*" I hollered, and slid off the cow, landing on my rump. The cow lumbered off down the creek bank.

"Durned old cow!" I picked up myself. "Durned stupid old cow! What's it laying in the middle of the road for, anyway?"

I guess Dora Faye couldn't help it, but she started laughing, and that made me mad. I took off up the road, huffing and snorting, calling her every name I could think of. I hurried right past her house and went over Copperhead Bridge at a gallop.

Mama was waiting.

She didn't look dangerous till I saw that hickory switch laying there beside her on the couch. Then I started talking as fast as I could, but I knew I was wasting my breath. Her expression didn't even change as she stood up and picked up the switch.

I glanced helplessly at Junie, but she was sitting there pretending to be all wrapped up in a book. I knew better. Mama grabbed me by the arm and began switching my bare legs, and I started dancing and squalling.

Each stripe she laid on my bare legs she punctuated with a word, like so: "*Dón't - yoú - éver - gó - oút - of -*

this - house - again - after - dárk - without - mé - ór - Júnie -
Dó - you - heár - mé? - Dó - you - heár - mé?"

"Yes, Mama! Yes, Mama, yes!"

"Now you get yourself to bed, and don't let me see your face again tonight!"

The most miserable of all humans, I climbed into bed, sore and sobbing. She was downright cruel. I would run away. Me and old Buddy would leave tonight after Mama and Junie were asleep. We wouldn't even take anything to eat. We would go up into the hills and live off the land. And next winter they'd find us cold and stiff up there in the snow. I'd have old Buddy dead in my dead arms, and they'd say, "That old dawg was the only one who ever loved this poor child."

She'd be sorry, then. She'd cry and wish she'd treated me better. Yes, that's what I'd do as soon as Mama and Junie were asleep. They would never see me alive again.

21

The sun was warm across my bed when I woke up. Mama and Junie were up and stirring already. Remembering the night before, I examined my injured legs and felt satisfied with the little red welts all wrapped around them. I made sure to wear shorts so Mama could see and be reminded every time she looked at me. Maybe she'd think twice before she ever struck me again.

Junie was tidying up the kitchen.

"Where's Mama?" I said, but she didn't answer.

"Is she gone to take that test already?"

No answer.

I sat down to cold biscuits and butter. That was probably where she was, I reckoned.

Junie was sweeping ashes out the back door. Already acting like Mama, I thought. Even wearing an apron. Bet she'd beat her kids someday, too. Not me. Never would I strike a precious child. I finished eating and wandered over to look out the window, thinking I'd slip off to Dora Faye's as soon as Junie turned her head. But Junie was making a big production out of cleaning my mess off the table where I had dropped crumbs and left a dirty dish. She slammed things down and flung her arms around a lot.

"Some people!" she said, her nose in the air. "Some people *never* clean up after their own self!"

That did it. I was off and up the hill, taking the short cut to Dora Faye's. But, to my disgust, Dora Faye was helping her mama can tomatoes. It seemed like that was all anybody thought of anymore—work!

Work! Then Dora Faye started laughing again and telling her mama about me falling on top of the cow, as if I wasn't already humiliated to the core. I started back home, deep in the mulligrubs.

I didn't want to face Junie again, so I crawled under the front porch with old Buddy. I didn't come out until I saw Mama walking up the road, but I didn't run to meet her and I didn't speak to her when she came in the gate.

"Ginny Carol," she said to me, just like nothing ever happened. "I want you to take that dog out to the creek directly and give him a good bath. He stinks."

"Okay . . . Didja take that test?"

I followed her up the steps and into the house.

"Yes."

"Was it hard?"

"Not very," she said. "Anyway, it was just me and Mrs. Moore and two real young girls. I know I did better than any of them."

Junie heard that.

"Miz Moore?" she said. "She took that test? Why, I bet she don't know a postcard from a money order!"

"Doesn't," Mama corrected her, smiling, seeming confident and happy.

"Why'd Miz Moore take the test?" I said, feeling uneasy. Wonder what that old vulture could be up to?

"I can't imagine," Mama said, and went into the kitchen to fix lunch. "With all her children, I don't see how she can even think of going to work. Her husband makes good money in the mines, anyway."

I was thinking of the evening before, how Mrs. Moore had said so hateful, "Is that a fact?" and "Well, la-di-da." Supposing she somehow messed up this chance for Mama, for all of us? Oh, why did I have to tell her, of all people?

After lunch Junie went over to borrow a dress pattern from Christine. Mama sat down on the couch with a new *Post*, and I sat across from her, hoping she'd see the stripes on my legs and apologize to me. Once in a while she glanced up at me over the top of her magazine. I tried to look as pitiful as I felt.

Finally, she laid the magazine down and stared at me long and hard. "Come here, Gin-Gin."

"What for?" I said, feeling the lump on my lip quiver a little. "You gonna beat me some more?"

I knew what was coming and I wanted to make it hard on her.

"No, come here and sit beside me."

I shuffled across the room and plopped down beside her sulkily.

She put an arm across my shoulder. "Gin, you know when I punish you it's for your own good. It's because I love you."

"Shucks!" I said. "I'd hate to see what you'd do to me if you didn't love me!"

She tried hard not to smile.

"It hurts me to whip you more than it hurts you," she went on.

"Then why ain't you got stripes all over *your* legs?" I said triumphantly, and raised one leg for her to see. I'd been rehearsing for that one because she always said that.

"They'll go away before you get married," she said, and patted my leg. "Now give me a kiss and go give that dog a bath."

I did as she said, feeling clean and light. Though my sins were as scarlet, she had washed them white as snow.

22

It was the end of the season for poke greens, sour grass, snake spit, tiger lilies, Queen Anne's lace, Indian paintbrushes, black-eyed Susans, daisies, dandelions, nettles, and witch doctors. It was the beginning of the season for milkweed pods, beechnuts, broomstraw, redbud, pawpaws, scaly barks and goldenrod, meaning it was growing toward the fall of the year.

Junie still wasn't very friendly with me, though she did break her vow not to speak to me, and Dora Faye was always helping her mama. It was then I decided Tildy may not be too bad to play with in a pinch. Anyway, she had no imagination a'tall and she thought everything I dreamed up was wonderful.

The first week of September found me and Tildy swinging on a grapevine on the hillside. All morning Tildy hummed to herself and sorta smiled, trying to be mysterious like she knew something she was dying to tell me. As aggravating as she was, I ignored her, because I knew what she wanted me to do was beg her to tell. Then she started chanting real low, "I know something I won't tell. I know something Ginny should know, but I won't tell." Still I ignored her, but it was getting harder.

Finally she couldn't stand my ignoring her anymore, and she said, almost in a whisper, "It's about that job your mama wanted so bad."

That did it.

"I bet your mama would skin you alive, Tildy," I said, "if she knew about you going all the way down to the mouth of the holler Saturday after she told you not to go."

"Who's gonna tell her?"

She could be so stupid.

"I am."

"You wouldn't do it."

"I would and I will if you don't spit it out right now what you know about that job."

"Why, what makes you think I know anything?"

"Here I go"—and I made out like I was going down the hill to tattle on her.

"All right. All right," she said. "Miz Moore got the job."

I was stunned. "Who told you that?"

"Miz Moore told Miz Mayfield, and Miz Mayfield told Miz Jenkins, and Miz Jenkins told my ma, and my ma told me."

"I don't believe it, Tildy Ratliff! You're a great big liar!"

"I am not! You go ask Ma! Ask anybody. Everybody knows!"

I wanted to cry with disappointment, but I would never cry, not in a million years, in front of Tildy. So instead I hit her right on the head with a big stick, and *she* cried. Then I took off down the hill, leaving her sitting there.

Mama was at the kitchen table shelling butter beans. I could tell by the look on her face she had heard the news already.

"Is it true, Mama?"

"Yes" was all she said.

So off I went to find old Buddy, my best friend and comforter.

The next day Mama took the bus to Richlands, to talk to some bigwig over at the post office. She had to know why. Junie moped around the house as silent as I don't know what, and I counted the hours till Mama would come home. At long last, toward evening, we saw her come poking up the road like she was wore out. Junie set supper on the table, and I ran to meet Mama. We didn't ask any questions till after we ate, and she didn't volunteer any answers.

Finally she settled down on the couch and sighed. "I guess you girls want to know what I found out."

We nodded.

"Well, I went to the man and I said to him, 'I have to know why this position was given to Mrs. Moore and not to me. I know very well I scored higher on the test than she did. I really need this job. My girls are growing up, and I can't give them the things they need with my Social Security check. There's no work for a woman in Sweet Creek Holler, and Mrs. Moore's husband is a miner. They aren't as needy as I am with my two girls. Doesn't the government care about people like us?'

"And the man said, 'I'm sorry, Mrs. Shortt, but this was a political appointment. That's just the way it is.'

"And I said, 'Political? But I voted for President Eisenhower. I am a Republican.'

"And he said, 'That's just it; you're a Republican. The state and local government is mostly Democratic. Mrs. Moore is a registered Democrat.' "

And that was that. Mrs. Moore said we'd pay. Well, I guess now she'd be satisfied. We knew she really didn't want or need this job; she just didn't want Mama to have it.

"Mrs. Moore called to me as I was coming up the road," Mama went on.

"What'd she say?" Junie asked.

"Well, she offered me a job. She said, 'Olivia, now that I'm working, I need somebody to wash my clothes and take care of my house and children. Think you could handle that?' "

"Don't do it!" me and Junie said together.

Mama sighed real long and hard, "I wouldn't, girls, but I honestly don't know how we're going to make it. I can't even buy you new clothes for school. You'll have to make do, I suppose, with last year's things for a while. Mrs. Moore said she'd pay me a dollar fifty a day."

"It don't matter!" Junie said, with tears in her eyes.

"Doesn't," Mama corrected her. "Hush now. It won't be forever. And it *is* a job."

Me and Junie hung our heads in shame. We knew

she was the best mama in Sweet Creek Holler, and too good to clean up Mrs. Moore's messes and look after her snotty-nosed kids.

On that note we went back to school the next week in our patched-up clothes.

23

I was still suffering with lovesickness for Junior Longridge. So the first day of school I was watching for him to top the hill up to the schoolhouse. I was standing around with a group of girls. We were in shoes for the first time in months, and trying not to scratch our heads.

Junior finally came strutting up the hill in his familiar black-and-white-checked jacket, and every female head turned his way. I thought I was going to upchuck, painfully aware that my feelings were shared by every girl at Sweet Creek Elementary— first grade through sixth. I watched Junior toss his jacket on the ground and join in a game of Round Town like an ordinary boy. He was totally ignorant of the fact that I had not died over the summer.

Nine o'clock found me sitting in Mrs. Mitchell's sixth-grade class with all the other sixth-graders, including Junior. In the back of my head a plan was slowly revolving. It had to be my year with Junior, I thought. He had claimed practically every girl in our class as his sweetheart in years gone by. It was time to do something magnificent to set me apart from all other girls and make Junior notice me. So the Sweet Creek Star Club was born.

The SCSC was to be a club for aspiring young starlets like myself who would write and perform plays for the entire school. It was no trouble at all getting my club together, since every girl in school wanted to be a star. Boys were something else again. They would rather play Round Town and Red Rover. Not to worry. They would see the finished product. I elected myself president first thing, then elected Dora Faye vice president and Susie Ruth secretary.

My first play was slapped together the weekend after school opened, and Monday recess found the SCSC trying out for parts in *Love's Eternal Bliss.*

I was soon drunk with power.

I could change lives with a nod of my head, meaning "Yes, you have the part," or "No, you won't do." And having every girl in school say, "Please, Ginny Carol, pick me for Elizabeth," or "I'll just die if I don't make it."

Naturally I got the part of Elizabeth, and my best friends got the other parts. There were grumblings and mutterings and general unrest until I smoothed things over by announcing there would be a whole new cast for the next play.

The following day we set about rehearsing *Love's Eternal Bliss*. It was a rambling, powerful drama, almost twenty minutes long, about two young women—me and Dora Faye—who were sisters and fell in love with the same man—Susie Ruth in her daddy's army uniform. Susie Ruth naturally loved me best, but I took the polio and was put in an iron lung, where I died of a broken heart. Susie Ruth turned to Dora Faye for consolation and, after much heartrending agony, decided to marry Dora Faye, even though she/he would always love me best. Susie Ruth even told Dora Faye how she/he still felt about me in the end, and Dora Faye said that was all right, because I was her beloved sister, and besides I was dead, so she didn't mind.

There wasn't a dry eye among us after that final scene, and even Tildy said I made better stories than the movies. I was tickled. It didn't seem quite so important about Junior anymore, because I was "hot."

The second day of rehearsal I got aggravated at the stage crew for whispering and giggling during our serious scenes, so I gave them a good lecture on respect for the stars. They looked at me sideways and went on talking. I decided to award parts in my next play to the ones who behaved best during rehearsal.

When I told them that, they settled down and tried to look interested.

The day after, I was biting my fingernails during geography and worrying about my club when the classroom door opened and in walked the most beautiful creature God ever placed on the face of the earth. She was a new student and she had long, black, shiny curls and dark, sparkling brown eyes and the face of an angel. I took one look at her and one look at Junior's face, and groaned in despair. And if that girl didn't have the moon and stars already, don't you think when Mrs. Mitchell asked her name she could have said "Mary Jane" or "Betty Lou" or something ordinary like that? But not this girl. Hang me if she didn't say "Melanie Rosalia Rambeau." I about died.

The injury to my lip never did heal up right. Though the scar was on the inside, an ugly lump showed on the outside, making my grins lopsided and my frowns bumpy. Before the world-shaking event of Melanie, I thought everybody else saw me like I saw myself—a cross between Judy Canova and Doris Day, depending on what mood I was in—and liked me as much as I liked myself. But suddenly it dawned on me that I had an ugly lip and lots of other flaws—like skinny knees, fingernails gnawed off to the knuckles (my fault), a long nose, wide flat feet, crooked teeth, and wrinkled elbows. Not to mention the fact that while Junie's hair had stayed a golden yella like Mama's, mine had turned brown and not a curl in sight. Puberty, also, was putting me off. Even the fifth-graders were ahead of me.

Not that I didn't like Melanie. Who wouldn't like a doll come to life? Just like everybody else in school, I was under her spell, but I couldn't help wondering how all that perfection got heaped up on one body while the rest of us got left out.

Those fall days I spent a lot of time looking at myself in the mirror. I used all my Doris Day faces— even some Elizabeth Taylor ones. I practiced holding the lump on my lip between my teeth to get it out of the way, but as soon as I opened my mouth, it popped out again. I did have dimples—one blessing to be thankful for. So I practiced holding my face just right to show off my dimples. Mama asked me if I had a toothache.

I tried rolling my hair in bobby pins at night—an awful ordeal. In the middle of the third night, I took all the bobby pins out and flung them on the floor, where some of them fell through the cracks, and it made Junie mad. She pointed out to me that, to her knowledge, bobby pins never had been found growing on trees, but "some people" didn't know things cost money.

Junior and Melanie claimed each other right off; it was written in the stars. It made me ache to watch them together. Naturally, Melanie was invited to join the SCSC the first day she took control of our world, and naturally the first meeting in her holy presence was total disaster. It seemed I no longer existed. All my orders were ignored. Things got no better as the days went by. *Love's Eternal Bliss* was sinking. All my efforts to save it seemed in vain.

"Okay," I hollered one day. "The next big mouth that interrupts the president of this club is henceforth and forever kicked out of the Sweet Creek Star Club."

Frowning but silent faces turned to me.

"Yeah," I said with more confidence. "Kicked out." I had their attention. Melanie put her hand over her mouth, which pleased me no end.

"Okay now. Let's get to work. Last time we were trying to begin Act II, but we never got nowhere. Susie Ruth, get up here!"

Susie Ruth didn't move.

"Now!" I stomped my foot at her.

There were dark rumblings and comments which I caught the tail end of: ". . . like a teacher" and "hateful" and "too bossy." I froze when I saw Tildy whispering to Melanie. I knew what she was saying, and I hated her for it.

"He gives 'em candy!" Melanie said, and my anger exploded.

I wanted to cry or scream or hit somebody.

Susie Ruth shuffled up beside me.

"Start where it says, 'My darling, my darling,'" I said, almost in tears.

"My darling, my darling . . ."

In the days to come, there were more and more whispers. Tildy had started it, and it spread like the itch. In the third week A.M. (After Melanie), I heard another whisper, "We want Melanie to be Elizabeth."

I was shattered, but what could I do?

Then Melanie said sweetly, "I think we should give the teachers a tea party after the play."

Nobody knew anything about giving tea parties, so nobody said anything.

"We could vote," she went on.

"Yeah, let's," Dora Faye said. "All in favor of giving the teachers a tea party after the play, raise your hand."

All hands went up—except mine.

"Done!" Dora Faye said, ignoring me.

I was completely unnerved that everybody wanted Melanie to be Elizabeth and that the tea-party idea didn't come from me. My club seemed to be going on its merry way with no help from me, and I was sure of only one thing: I was being ignored.

"It has to be unanimous," I said sulkily.

Everybody groaned.

"Well, if you don't like it . . ." I groped for the right words. "Just . . . just get out of my club!"

No sooner said than done. I was dethroned.

24

I fancied October was my own special time. There were days when I drifted, aimless and dreamy. I became a part of the woods, like a leaf in autumn floating to earth, never landing. The future was suspended before me like stars in a black night, and the past was beginning to take shape like a road map that had led me to this point.

There began a pain in my chest too big for my little body but too heavy to get rid of. It started when the SCSC removed me and went on without me. But it deepened when I tried to wade through Thomas Wolfe's *Look Homeward, Angel* and didn't understand half of what I read. I just knew he was describing my pain and I couldn't decipher his meaning. His one line "O lost, and by the wind grieved, ghost, come back again" took hold of me like nothing ever did before.

"Oh, what does it mean?" I agonized. "And why does it hurt me so bad?"

I asked Mrs. Mitchell what it meant, and she said, "Ginny, what in the world are you reading that for? Don't you know it's too hard for you?"

So I asked my mama, who knew everything, and she said, "I don't know, but isn't it lovely?"

What did it mean, and why did it hurt me so bad? It meant a yearning for something, didn't it? But what? I didn't know what I yearned for, either. I felt there would always be this pain. It was a mourning, a grief for something lost.

I felt the pain when I watched the golden autumn leaves and the cliffs washed by the Appalachian sunset, as I listened to the sounds of the birdcalls and smelled the mossy streams. I felt the pain of the earth as its summer died . . . the fragrances of the earth and the long, lost cries of the wild things searching for a mate. Then there were the cold painful mornings when I felt my life was fragile, and there were songs made by the wind in the lonesome pines . . . the evening light on the bark of a tree . . .

"What's wrong with you, Ginny Carol Shortt?" I would chastise myself. "You think too much!"

But the pain went on.

I was alone. Mama was always busy with work, Junie was too grown-up and too pigheaded to play with me anymore, and every girlfriend I ever had belonged to the SCSC. I hated every boy in the world, including Junior Longridge. It was truly a melancholy time.

One Friday I was absent from school with a sudden bellyache. *Love's Eternal Bliss* was to be performed that day, with Melanie Rosalia Rambeau in the lead. I reckoned there should be a law protecting writers from such thievery. And the tea party was also going on as planned.

But I had old Buddy. That evening, me and old Buddy went up into the hills together for one of our ramblings. He sure was happy. He grinned at me and didn't just wag his tail; he wagged all over. I sure loved that old dog. He sure was sweet.

We walked a long, long time through the woods. The only sound was our feet crunching the dead leaves. I was thinking of nothing in particular when all of a sudden there was Lou Jean just sitting there in a pile of leaves, holding a lighted match to her apron hem. She was so intent on what she was doing she didn't even hear me and old Buddy. She looked funny—her face pale, and her seeming so small and weak, with her tummy all stuck out. There were black holes all over her apron where she'd held matches to it.

"What in thunderation you doin'?" I couldn't help hollering.

She jumped clear off the ground and gasped as her

head shot toward me. Her eyes were wild. She shook the match hard and tossed it away.

"No . . . nothing," she said, like she was out of breath. "What . . . who . . . ? Oh, Ginny Carol, you scairt me most to death."

"What've you done to your apron?" I said.

"Oh, oh, this old thing?" She gave the scarred apron a flip. "I . . . I was trying to burn it up. Ain't worth nothing . . . Just felt like burning it up." Her voice trailed away.

"Well, don't you think you should take it off first?"

She just stared at me.

"You could catch yourself afire," I said.

The way her eyes glazed over made me uneasy.

"What you doing all the way up here by yourself, Lou Jean?"

She sat back down all the way and her tummy lay out bold and startling before her. "Will went to the army," she said.

"Yeah, I heard."

"But it's his."

"The baby, you mean?"

"Yeah, the baby's Will's. God knows it is."

I didn't know what to say.

She pulled a big box of kitchen matches from her apron pocket and studied it with great interest. "They say old Hitler burned all them people in the war," she said softly. "You think that's really true?"

"I reckon so."

"Reckon they felt anything?"

"Who? Oh, the people old Hitler burned? I don't know."

"I bet they did. I bet they felt like they was in hell. I bet the pain was so bad you can still hear their screams if you know where to listen. I bet . . ."

"Shucks, Lou Jean, what'd you wanta think of that for?"

"If I'd been a good girl . . ." she said. "If only I'd been a good girl like Ma and Pa taught me to be . . . then they wouldn't be back there at the house crying. Both of them are crying, even Pa, and he's drunk again, too. He didn't drink for . . . well, for months, and today he got drunk again, all because of me."

"What's the matter?"

"It's what folks are saying. They're saying my pa is unnatural. They're saying he likes young girls. Now they're saying I got my baby from Pa and packed it off on Will Jenkins."

My stomach turned over. Hate welled up in me, and there was nowhere to spit it out except at Lou Jean. "Shut up, Lou Jean! That's the wickedest thing I ever heard. You made it up!"

"No!" Her eyes were bright with a terrible excitement. "It's what they're saying—Miz Moore and all of them. It's all my fault. I should burn in hell. I was so bad!"

My anger faded and I was overwhelmed with pity for her. I sat down beside her on the leaves. "Oh, Lou, I'm sorry I yelled at you. I didn't mean it. You ain't done nothing, Lou. You're the best person I know. You just loved Will so much, I know that, Lou."

She smiled a little then and put her arm around me. "And what brings you up here all by yourself? I never saw you by yourself before. You always had a passel of friends."

"Not anymore," I said sadly, feeling very sorry for myself. "Everybody hates me now."

"That kain't be so. You're so sweet, Ginny."

"Oh, Lou Jean." I burst into tears, overcome by my own loneliness and pain, and suddenly having a friend to listen to me.

"Tell me about it, Ginny."

And it all tumbled out of me—about Mama having to work for Mrs. Moore and never having time for me anymore, about Junie being mad at me since midsummer on account of I jerked her petticoats off at the fair, and about all my friends at school kicking me out of my own club and using my play just like it was theirs. She listened to it all, holding me in her arms and patting me like I was a little bitty baby. So, in the end, even in her own grief and shame, it was Lou Jean who comforted me, as we sat there in friendship once again in October's golden leaves.

25

On the first day of Christmas vacation the punch-board I had ordered arrived in the mail. I thought I would set off to sell chances the next morning, early, up and down the holler.

Then it started snowing. We didn't get a lot of snow in the middle of December, and we hoped it would lay for Christmas. It was dark by five-thirty, and we huddled around Mama on the old blue couch with rugs wrapped around our feet while she read to us from *Little Women*.

After a while Mama got tired of reading and started listening to *Beulah* on the radio, and I helped her listen. Suddenly there was a *knock! knock! knock!* real loud on the door. Mama hurried to answer it, and Poppy was blown in with a gust of wind and snow.

"Lordy, what a night!" he boomed as Mama closed the door behind him. "How's about a kiss for poor ole Poppy!"

I hugged him and kissed him, and he handed me a poke of candy. Junie sat still and didn't look at him, but he didn't even notice, and I shared the candy with Junie, anyway.

Poppy settled down on a chair and wanted to know how we were doing in school, and if we'd had any whoopings lately, and if our poor old daddy would be proud of us or ashamed if he was here to see. It was agreed that Daddy would be proud.

"How come it's so cold in here?" Poppy wanted to know all of a sudden.

"It's always cold in here," Junie said.

"Well, is the heatin' stove puttin' out like it orta?" he said.

"Nothing wrong with the heatin' stove," Junie said in a smart-aleck voice. "It's because we don't have any insulation in this house," Junie went on, bold as could be. "You can feel the cold just whistling through the walls and up through the cracks in the floor. Every winter, you tell us you're gonna insulate and underpin this house, but you never do!"

"Junie!" Mama said, her face red. "That is not your poppy's responsibility! He's done more than enough for us, just out of the goodness of his heart."

"Then he shouldn't say he's gonna do something, when he don't mean to do it a'tall! Just like he's always saying he's gonna come see us and he don't hardly ever do it! And we miss him!"

Junie got tears in her eyes.

"And when he does come," she choked, "he can't wait to get away!"

A horn blew out front. Poppy got a funny look on

his face, but he didn't say a word. Junie left the room, her eyes overflowing.

None of us said anything for a long time. I thought Poppy was going to cry, too, but he didn't.

"Well, I gotta go," he said abruptly. "Ginny, you mind your mama now."

Then he was gone into the night again. From the window I saw a jeep close him inside. I didn't know who brought him forth on such a night or when, if ever, he would come again. But I felt like he would not be back for a long, long time. What I did know, with a melancholy ache, was that my world was changing. Nothing would ever be the same again.

Tucked snugly in bed beside Mama, I came awake near dawn and saw the first dim light filter through the snow and reach our bedroom. It was snowing real hard. It didn't make a sound as it wrapped us closer into our sheltered valley. The approaching light, the silent snow, the sound of my mother's and sister's breathing in the ice-cold bedroom, the great silence, all this swept through me in great lonely waves. I felt that longing . . . that yearning for what? The early-morning train rumbled through the valley, echoed between the hills, then died away. Where was it going? Where had it been? What kind of world lay beyond these hills? Would I ever see it? I thought about Shirley Clancy and wondered if she ever thought these thoughts? The past and the future blended. I became one with that long-ago little girl. The train whistle gave one last mournful cry, and I shuddered, snuggling close to Mama, my rock.

Next morning I wrapped up warm as toast in preparation for going up the holler to sell chances on my punchboard. I figured Junie wanted to go, too, but was too proud to say so. I decided to ask her right out, "Wanna come along?"

"And who do you think is gonna clean up the house if I go trotting off to have a good time?" she said, real sharp.

"Well, I just asked!" I answered. My feelings were hurt. "I don't care if you go or not!"

I set off up the road, feeling isolated from my sister, who used to be my good friend. Seemed like everything we said to each other these days rubbed the wrong way. I wished we could be friends again.

Old Buddy went with me. He never let me down.

I had three pairs of socks on my hands, but soon they were wet all the way through where I played in the snow, and my fingers got numb. The sun was cold and white. The mountains rose in white splendor all around. I wound my way up the valley. I stopped at the Ratliffs', the Esteps', the Looneys', and other families far up the holler, while old Buddy sat waiting outside for me. Nearly everybody liked punchboards, and nearly everybody bought a chance. The prize was to be a bright rhinestone necklace with fifty white and thirty red stones, all set in six rows. It was a masterpiece. I had gazed at it in *Modern Romances* for days before I finally talked Mama into letting me order the punchboard. She said I could get it for Christmas. The punchboard company would send me a dollar for selling the chances.

It was exciting to go into each house, unwrap my hands, and show them my board, along with a picture of the beautiful necklace. Everybody oohed and aahed over the necklace, then invited me to warm my hands by the heatin' stove. I felt sharp tingles in my hands as the heat seeped in. When they hurt too bad, I would stick my fingers in my mouth.

My nose ran and I wiped it on my coat sleeve, but nobody noticed as they deliberated over the little perforated circles on the punchboard. Which one to punch?

"Punch this one, Mommy," the children would say.

"No! Forty-nine! Forty-nine looks like a winner."

And when the choice was made, we all stood holding our breath as the little circle was punched out with a pencil point, and the number inside was revealed. They all groaned if $1.04 showed up, and squealed with delight at 19¢. Anything around 50¢ wasn't too bad.

With the right amount paid and slipped into my Rosebud salve box, I wrapped my hands up tight again, left amid cheerful goodbyes and reminders to "be sure and let us know who wins."

Then I plodded through the snow to the next house.

I couldn't decide whether or not I should go to the Purvises', not so much on account of Lou Jean's baby boy, who was a few weeks old, but on account of Mrs. Purvis. I finally decided to go. After all, to my knowledge, Mrs. Purvis never had murdered anybody.

Getting up the hill was the hard part because I kept sliding back down, but I finally managed and found myself knocking on the door. Mrs. Purvis answered and I wished right away I hadn't bothered to come. She was so frizzy-headed it seemed like the rats could nest in her hair. She was dirty, and she towered over me.

"What is it?" she said, sour as could be.

I explained what I came for as best I could with her frowning down at me, but it wasn't easy. Silently, she opened the door wider and stood aside for me to go in. I couldn't help feeling entombed the minute she closed the door behind me, because that was the dirtiest, darkest room I ever entered, and there was a smell that just about emptied my stomach. I bet the roaches thought they had died and gone to heaven there.

"Set down and warm your hands." She motioned me to a rocking chair by the heatin' stove.

I handed her the punchboard and the picture of the necklace. I glanced around the room, and lo and behold, what I thought was just a piece of furniture over by the window turned out to be Lou Jean. I couldn't see her face because she had her back to me, and she didn't even turn around when I said, "Hidy, Lou Jean."

She was tending the baby, which I heard making gurgling sounds, but I couldn't see him. Lou Jean was huddled low over him. I remembered the candy party in this same room. That was on a summer day over five years ago, and all the doors and windows were open. The place and the people were so clean that day, who'd ever think they would come to this dismal scene? And the laughter . . . everybody was laughing that day—even Mrs. Purvis because it was a special occasion to give a party for her pretty Lou Jean. I shivered, wishing Mrs. Purvis would hurry up.

"Don't reckon I'd have any use for a necklace like that," she finally said.

"That's okay," I said quickly. "Don't everybody care for necklaces."

"That's a fact," she said and handed the board and the picture back to me. "Yeah, that's a fact."

"Okay, well, I'll be going now, I reckon."

I shuffled toward the door, glancing toward Lou Jean. She hadn't moved.

"Don't hurry off," Mrs. Purvis said without enthusiasm. It's something everybody said in Sweet Creek Holler, whether they meant it or not. She was studying her dirty fingernails.

"Reckon I better go," I said. "S'long, Lou Jean."

There was no answer from her.

I was out the door in a jiffy, breathing deeply of the fresh air. I reckoned I never wanted to go inside that house again. Me and old Buddy half walked, half fell down the hill onto the footbridge and into the road. The Clancy house was before me. About that time Josh Clancy came out on the front porch and looked around his yard at the snow.

"Hidy, Mr. Clancy," I hollered, and he sorta tipped his hat to me.

I couldn't ask Josh Clancy to buy a chance on a punchboard. Nobody ever had before. Nobody ever included the Clancys in anything. Who'd ever think to ask Mrs. Clancy to a bean stringin'? She probably wouldn't go, anyway, but Josh was right friendly sometimes.

I stopped in the road and thought: Heck, why not?

"Wanna buy a chance on a punchboard?"

He turned toward me and cupped his hand over his ear.

"Punchboard!" I hollered again and held up the board.

He still didn't understand, and he motioned for me to come closer. Breathless, I set out across that wide expanse of clean snow, feeling like I was tracking up somebody's clean floor.

"You wanna buy a chance on a punchboard?" I said again when I was near him.

At first he looked like he wondered how I had the nerve to bother him with such stuff. I wondered my own self. He was tremendous up close. He had these huge wide shoulders and enormous hands, and he was way over six feet tall.

Sighing, he pulled a pipe out of his pocket. "What's the prize?" he asked, just like everybody else.

I breathed easier and held up a picture of the necklace.

"Guess not." He grinned. "I have nothing to match it."

I laughed a little. "Reckon not," I said. "How about your mama? She might like it."

"I think not, Gin . . . is it Ginny?"

"Ginny Carol Shortt," I said.

"Yes, Ginny Carol Shortt. And how is your mother?" He smiled again.

"Fine, I reckon."

Then I swallowed hard, because standing right there inside the door looking out one of those little windows running down the side of the door was the witch. She was looking right at me.

Josh Clancy's eyes followed mine, because I guess I was gaping.

Mrs. Clancy tapped on the glass and wiggled her finger at Josh to "come here." I sorta backed off as Josh opened the door and talked to his mama in low tones.

"Wait." He turned back to me. "How much is a chance?"

Well, blow me down.

"Anywhere from 19¢ to $1.04. You punch first. That tells you how much to pay."

"Well, give me all the rest," he said, just like that, and held out a five-dollar bill in his big hand.

I was flustered. I would have to punch out each circle, add them up, and change that big old five while him and the witch stood there watching me. I'd never make it.

"Come on," Mr. Clancy said. "Just punch the circles and take the five. It will cover all the rest of the chances."

Nervously I punched the circles into his hand, took the bill, mumbled "Thank you," and turned tail.

I was on the road when I heard him start the truck by the front door. I was thinking, Junie will never believe this.

It was then I heard the most awful sound of my

whole life, and every ounce of me turned weak. It was old Buddy. He cried one mournful, terrible cry, then a sickening silence pounded in my ears. I saw Josh Clancy climb back out of his truck and bend down on the ground; then he looked at me. I knew. I think I ran screaming toward him, but the next while was all a blur and I'm not sure if he carried me or dragged me into the house. And I could hear my own screams like echoes from a nightmare right there in the Clancy house while the old witch bent over me, and Josh seemed so pitiful, and I didn't care about any of it a'tall, because the best dog in Virginia was dead.

26

It was late in the afternoon when I joined the world of the living again. At first I thought I was still asleep and dreaming. There was this sound of lots and lots of clocks ticking in my head. *Tick-tock. Tick-tock.* My eyes flew open. Real high ceiling. A chandelier. A room all rose-colored and faded pink. A portrait of two little girls over a fireplace. Lenora and Shirley! I was in the rose room! The very room I had dreamed about all those times. And there were the clocks,

mayby fifty of them, lined up on shelves covering
one whole wall. I was on a rose-colored couch so soft
it felt like I might sink right through. There was no
fire in the fireplace and not a heatin' stove in sight,
but the room was real warm, which was a curiosity to
think on—but later.

I was alone in the room, though I had a feeling
someone had just left. I sat up, too dazed at first to
remember exactly why I was here; then it hit me like
a blow directly to my heart.

Old Buddy!

I vaguely remembered having had a warm liquid
forced down my throat before everything faded away
and merciful sleep dulled my first pangs of grief.
Now my head was fuzzy and the room seemed to be
floating in front of my eyes.

I felt one terrible emotion—bitterness. Never,
never, would I ever forgive Josh Clancy for killing
my dog—never. Tears stung my eyes. That sweet old
dog—crushed. I heard that lonesome train whistle in
the back of my mind. I would hear it forever . . .
forever . . . whenever a loved one would leave me.
Yes, they would all leave—like Daddy, like Buddy,
Mama and Junie would leave me someday, too. Poppy
and Granny and my friends—they had already left
me in a way; Lou Jean, too.

With the rose room swimming before me, a real
funny feeling came over me. It seemed like the clocks

all stopped or faded out of earshot, and a big blazing fire suddenly sprang up in the fireplace where none was before. I gasped, but before the sound was out of my throat good, I was distracted by something else even more eerie. It made me tremble. The front door to my left gave the illusion of opening and closing, though it really didn't do it at all, and in came the two ghost girls all bundled up in heavy coats, boots, 'boggans, and mittens. They sat down on the same couch where I was sitting, so close I had to move to keep them from sitting on top of me! They were laughing and jabbering about a snowball fight, and they started peeling off their heavy clothes and throwing them right on top of me!

Maybe they couldn't see me. But I declare I could feel and smell the wet wool of their coats, and the snow coldness coming off them. I got up and moved back to look at them.

"I'm here," I said in a trembly little voice, but they went on cutting up.

Maybe they couldn't hear me, either.

"I'm here," I said again louder, but they ignored me.

So I just watched and listened, my heart thundering.

Then, just like the scene changes in a movie sometimes, this scene changed right in front of my eyes. The wet wool things were gone, the fireplace was cold again, and the littlest girl, Shirley, was stretched out on the couch in a pink nightgown with a sheet pulled up to her chin. The big girl, Lenora, was crying and kneeling on the floor beside her with her hand laid on Shirley's forehead.

"Shirley, Papa's gone for the doctor. You'll feel better when the doctor comes. Will you please eat a little now?"

Shirley shook her head. I noticed her face was pale and her eyes had dark rings under them. Shirley looked at me then. She did! She saw me!

"Who is that girl, Lenora?"

Lenora looked my way, but she did not see me.

"What girl?"

Shirley pointed at me.

"Right there! Can't you see her? There's a girl there. I think I know her."

Lenora looked so sad. "There's nobody there, Shirley. You're delirious."

"Will you read to me, Lenora?"

"Of course. What would you like to hear?"

"The Secret Garden."

Lenora stood up and left the room, to fetch the book, I reckoned.

"You'll like *The Secret Garden*," Shirley said, and smiled at me.

"Yeah, my mother read it to me when I was little," I said. But she was gone!

The couch was bare again, and a heavy, sickening odor of flowers came over me so suddenly I about gagged. Death! It smelled like death! Daddy's funeral came back to me . . . and something more . . . much more.

I whirled around to look into the darker corners of the rose room, and to my horror there were two caskets draped in flowers, and inside them were the two girls.

"Ginny!"

Junie walked up behind me and touched my shoulder, and I about fainted.

I came back to the present with such a jolt I had to grab onto Junie to keep from falling down. She eased me onto the couch. The clocks all started ticking again, the caskets and flowers were gone, and I was shaking all over. Junie put her arm around me as she sat down beside me, and I looked away because I didn't want her to see the tears in my eyes.

"Oh, Ginny." Junie's voice quivered.

I looked at her then. There were tears in her eyes, too.

"I've been busting to tell you," she said, "ever since Josh Clancy fetched me and Mama in the truck. I even said it out loud, but you were asleep."

Tears were pouring down her cheeks. "I'm sorry— that's what I wanted to say. I'm sorry I was so mean to you. I know you never meant to jerk my petticoats

off at the fair. And I'm sorry about old Buddy, too.
I loved him, too, but not like you did. I'm sorry about
everything—and I'm sorry about your club at school.
They were mean to you."

I hated Junie knowing about my club. It made my
face burn. And after all her pretty apologies I was
mad, knowing she knew about that.

"No matter whatever happens from now on, you
. . . you're my little sister, and I love you."

She choked on the last words and I felt sorry for
her. I was sorry about everything, too, but I couldn't
say it right then. I felt drained, and very, very sad. I
slumped back on the couch and closed my eyes. I
reckoned nothing else would ever matter very much
again . . . Old Buddy!

"Junie," I said softly. "This is the room."

"I know," she said. "I recognized it as soon as I
saw it, and I saw the ghost girls going up the stairs—
twice."

That's what I loved about Junie. You didn't have
to explain a lot of things to her. It was like our minds
worked together. And she took everything I said as
gospel. Then I told her all the things I saw in the
rose room, and by the time I finished about the
caskets and all, we were both crying so hard we
couldn't speak for a while. We just sat together and
looked around the room, wondering why and how
these visions came to us.

"Where's Mama?" I said at last.

"In the kitchen with Miz Clancy. They been talking up a storm just like old friends. I never saw the beat. There we couldn't get a word outta Mama to strangers for years. Now you can't get a word in sideways."

"Mama and the witch?"

"Shh . . . Ginny," Junie whispered. "She's no witch! She's a nice lady. I reckon her and Mama hit it off. Miz Clancy is making tea and cookies now."

"And here they are," Mrs. Clancy said, real cheerful-like as she came in the room with a tray holding a teapot and these little bitty cups. Mama was right behind her with a tray of cookies. She set her tray down and kissed me. I about cried again, but I didn't.

"Didn't you work for the old vulture today, Mama?"

"Yes, but I took the afternoon off," she said and handed me a cookie. "I figured my girls needed me."

"Tell her what happened, Mama," Junie said with a grin.

"Well," Mama started her story. "Mrs. Moore was home for lunch when Josh drove up. I went out to see what he wanted; then I went back into Mrs. Moore's house to get my things together to leave.

"And Mrs. Moore said to me, 'Just where do you think you're going to, Olivia Shortt?'

"And I said to her, 'I have to go to the Clancys'.' It didn't occur to me until later what effect those words had on Mrs. Moore. She was actually speechless for the first time in her life."

Everybody busted out laughing then, even Mrs. Clancy, and I thought to myself: Self, you can do it. You can laugh, too.

And I did.

"But I guess I lost my job," Mama went on.

"Good!" me and Junie said together.

"I'd ruther wear feed-sack dresses and eat fried possums than have you work for that woman anymore!" I said.

Mrs. Clancy laughed at that one. "Maybe you won't have to eat fried possums, Ginny," she said to me, smiling. "Your mother can work for me if she wants to. This old house is big enough for three or four women to look after."

We were all wondering if she was serious, when she set our minds at ease.

"It's true. It would only be for a couple of months because we're moving back to Pennsylvania in the spring. But in the meantime there's lots of packing and cleaning out and throwing away that needs to be done. Josh doesn't have the time to help me. He's so busy trying to sell the mines and keep them in good shape at the same time."

"You're leaving?" Junie said.

"Yes." Mrs. Clancy sighed. "It's time, my dear. We should have left fifteen years ago. There are too many unpleasant memories here. It's time to put them all behind us and start living in the present again instead of the past."

We knew she was talking about the two little girls and her husband, who killed them, but we didn't say anything. Wouldn't it be great fun to ramble through all Mrs. Clancy's stuff?

"We could help," I said.

"And so you could," Mrs. Clancy agreed. "Now, Miss Ginny, let's see who won that gorgeous necklace on the punchboard."

Mama punched out the master circle and Mrs. Clancy was declared the winner. When she turned around and said I should have the necklace, I knew I was going to like her for sure. With the dollar I earned selling the chances and whatever Josh overpaid, and now the necklace on top of all that, I thought maybe life could be worth living again.

We went home late and had fried chicken for supper. Mama tried to talk to me about forgiving Josh.

"He felt bad about it, Ginny," she said to me. "You know he didn't do it on purpose. You must tell him you don't blame him."

I didn't say anything.

Later, I tried to help Mama and Junie clean up the kitchen without their even asking me to. But when we scraped all the plates, I looked at the leftovers and thought, Boy! What a treat for old Buddy! And this sick feeling came over me again. I crawled away to bed, knowing it was going to hurt for a long time.

27

Those days of helping Mrs. Clancy were about the most fun me and Junie ever had. Mama went early every morning, and me and Junie went after school and on weekends. Even though the grown-ups did all the hard work and put me and Junie in the kitchen to do the cooking, it was fun when we got together for meals. Mrs. Clancy had a freezer where she kept all kinds of meat, and she had hundreds of cans of store-bought stuff and a refrigerator full of fresh fruits and vegetables. She also had an electric stove and running hot water right in her kitchen. We looked up recipes and fixed something different every day. Junie was a good cook. I just helped her do things like peel vegetables, find ingredients and set them out for her, and clean up. We were growing close again.

Sometimes when Junie and I walked into a room, we both had the feeling someone had just left that room, even though Mama and Mrs. Clancy were somewhere else in the house entirely. It was a rush of air or a whiff of some smell we didn't quite recognize, or a movement caught at the corner of our eyes. Junie and I would look at each other at these times. We both felt the ghost girls were there, around the corner or behind a door, or ready to enter the room, but we never really saw them during this happy period of our lives.

Mama was having fun, too. She and Mrs. Clancy spent hours together talking and laughing as they sorted through mountains of old clothes, household items, pictures and documents. Mrs. Clancy gave us lots of things she said she didn't need anymore but we sure could use.

Josh was pleased his mama had a friend. At first he passed through the house ever once in a while and hollered, "Hi," and went on his way to his mines. But I didn't look at him or speak. He killed my dog and I wasn't going to forget or forgive. But then it got so he would hang around for a while. He helped Mama and Mrs. Clancy or he came into the kitchen and carried on some foolishness with me and Junie. He started telling us funny stories, and I couldn't help laughing even when I tried not to.

Like once he told us he knew a family in Pennsylvania whose last name was Lear. "They had a girl first," he said, "and they named her Crystal Chanda. Then they had a boy and named him Gay Cava."

"Is that the truth?" Junie said, laughing.

"So help me," Josh said. "Ask my mother. She knew them, too."

"That's right," Mrs. Clancy said, as she and Mama came into the kitchen. "I don't know what he's talking about, but I never argue with Josh. You can't win."

Everybody laughed.

"What's for supper, Junie?" Mrs. Clancy asked, sniffing the air.

"Broiled shad with lemon sauce and Chinese vegetables," Junie said excitedly, clapping her hands together.

Mama smiled. She was proud of Junie.

Mrs. Clancy looked around the kitchen at the mess. "Well, it should be good." She grinned. "Looks like you used up every utensil in the house."

"You know we'll clean it up. Come on into the dining room and set down," I said.

"*Sit!*" Mama said. "*Sit* down, Ginny."

"Right. *Sit* down," I said, and Josh winked at me. But I turned away.

We all sat around the enormous dining-room table and filled up our plates without saying much. Junie couldn't wait for the grown-ups to try her special recipes.

"Miz Clancy," I said. "I been meaning to ask you something. How come y'all kept them old horses?"

"You mean Wee, Willie, and Winkie?"

"That their names?"

"Yes, the horses belonged to my children—Shirley, Lenora, and Josh. They were purchased by my husband, Tom, shortly before the girls died. They were beautiful horses then. But they grew old and cranky. Still, I didn't have the heart to get rid of them. Josh finally gave them away to some people he knows in Richlands after they scared some little girl half out of her wits."

Mama, Junie, and Josh were all grinning at me. I ducked my head.

"It was that little girl's mother I didn't want to tangle with," Josh said, grinning at Mama. "She sure gave me a piece of her mind."

Mama was blushing. Her eyes met Josh's across the table. He was teasing her, and for the first time I detected some kind of chemistry between my mama and Josh. I couldn't believe it. How could my own mama like a man who killed old Buddy?

We were all going around for second helpings.

"My goodness, June Marie, this is delicious," Mrs. Clancy said, and Junie beamed.

"I guess your children liked the horses?" I went on, hoping Mrs. Clancy would talk more about the girls.

"Lenora and Josh loved them and loved riding. But poor Shirley, the baby, was frightened to death of them. But she tried just the same, bless her heart.

She would ride right along with the others, even though she was terrified. They liked to go out very, very early in the morning before it got too hot. They would ride up and down the road and into the hills. Then they would come home all exhilarated and apple-cheeked, and eat the biggest breakfast you ever saw. I don't know where they put it all."

Mrs. Clancy was smiling as she remembered happier times. "In fact, they were out riding that morning when they found the little Purvis girl in the mining shaft, isn't that right, Josh?"

"Lou Jean!" Junie and me said together. "In a mining shaft!"

"Yes," Josh said. "She was just under a year old. Her father was supposed to be watching her, but he got drunk and passed out. The mother was off at some church conference or something. Anyway, Lou Jean crawled off from the house—she couldn't even walk—and she fell into a mining shaft over there on the hill. It's been filled since then. It wasn't very deep, but to a baby it must have seemed like a deep black pit."

"Why, Ginny Carol, that reminds me of a nightmare you had one time, remember?" Mama said.

I nodded. How could I forget?

"So we were riding by," Josh continued, "and we heard a baby crying. We followed the sound and there was Lou Jean as black as a little black baby from coal dust, peeping out of that hole. I climbed down and pulled her out."

"Why, anything could have happened to that poor child," Mrs. Clancy said. "Always after that, my Lenora and Shirley just loved that baby. They took care of her all they could. I think they felt responsible for Lou Jean after that."

"It seems to me I rescued Lou Jean from another narrow escape some years later," Josh said, real sneaky-like, and looked at me.

"Did anybody ever ride the horses again?" I interrupted him loudly. I knew he was thinking of the day Lou Jean was swinging on the grapevine and it broke. Josh was grinning again. He sure loved to tease.

"No," Mrs. Clancy said. "Josh went back to boarding school in Pennsylvania that autumn, and Lenora couldn't get Shirley to ride anymore. Then my girls . . ." Mrs. Clancy seemed agitated. "Josh . . . Josh would exercise the horses sometimes back in the hills, but no, they were never ridden again. When I went to take Josh back to school, my girls . . . my girls came down with typhoid. They died shortly after that."

Mrs. Clancy dropped her fork. Mine and Junie's eyes met and locked.

Typhoid fever!

Mama patted Mrs. Clancy's shoulder.

"You okay, Mom?" Josh asked.

"I'm all right." She managed a smile. "I can talk about it now. Years went by, Olivia, I wouldn't accept it had really happened. You see, I was the learned lady from the North. I should have known better."

"Known better than what?" Junie said. "What happened?"

"I mean, I let my girls play in that filthy creek. It reeks with typhoid. All the local children are immunized every year against typhoid fever. So there you have it. The learned lady from the North didn't know everything. For years I pretended it didn't happen, that they were still here with me. They were so real sometimes I could see them plain as day."

Junie and I exchanged another meaningful look.

"As long as I stayed in the house and didn't see other people's children, I could keep the illusion alive. So I shut myself away from the world with my craziness.

"Then something happened. Do you remember that day, Ginny, when you and Junie came to ask me for old catalogues?"

"Sure."

"Well, when I saw you two standing there, it was the craziest thing. There was something about you that reminded me of my girls. And this wild hope went through me that somehow my girls had actually returned to me. I was watching every move you made that day—when you went down in the cellar and when you came back up laughing so hard, and you were all loaded down with old catalogues. And I found I was laughing, too, and crying a little, too. And it made me so happy to give you girls pleasure. I thought what a simple thing it was to make somebody else happy.

"I couldn't think of anything else for a long time. I thought how good it feels to reach out after so many years and do something for somebody else. And I thought I could do a lot of things for people if I would just come out of my shell.

"Then when you came with the punchboard, you looked so cold, Ginny, I wanted to buy all your chances so you could go home and warm up. You looked like my little Shirley standing there, so little and cold in the snow."

I felt like crying. Mama and Junie had tears in their eyes. Josh had put down his fork and was looking out the window over Mama's head.

"And now it seems the heartache isn't half so hard to bear since you are here. It's time to let go of the past."

All those years, I thought, we were afraid of her and called her a witch, but she was just a lonely old woman who had lost her little girls. How many people, I thought, might have secret sorrows like hers, and we misunderstand them and misjudge them?

"What happened to Mr. Clancy?" Junie asked.

"Don't ask any more questions, Junie," Mama said.

"That's all right, Olivia. I don't mind," Mrs. Clancy said. "My husband was so stricken with grief, he sat over the coffins for hours with a gun, threatening to kill anyone who tried to put them in the ground. It was an awful time. Then Josh, bless his heart, talked his father into giving up the gun and going to bed. But the poor man couldn't bear the grief. He never could cope with emotional pain. He shot himself a few weeks later."

Now there was a story, I thought, that really went haywire in Sweet Creek Holler. The facts had become so twisted that all folks remembered was Tom Clancy with a gun. They said he killed his own children, then his own self. Were people so starved for excitement that they wanted to believe something as awful as that?

"Josh was only sixteen at the time. He came home and tried to pick up the pieces. He took over everything he could at the time, and he took on more and more as the years went by. He's been a rock of strength to me. But I have not been fair to him. He has sacrificed so much for me—his education, good times, girlfriends."

Josh shuffled around uncomfortably and took a big gulp of coffee.

"It's time he started living, too. He wants an engineering degree. So I'm going to send him back to school next autumn. He's only thirty-one. It's never too late."

"Mama's thirty-one, too," Junie said absently, and a long moment of silence followed. I knew everybody at the table but me was playing matchmaker at that moment.

So that was the story of the Clancys.

It was dark when we went home that night, and Mama walked us down the road with an arm around each of us. I felt like we were a real family again.

Then we heard singing.

Open door, open arms
Wait for your safe return.

"It's poor Lou Jean," Mama said, and we all stopped and looked toward the Purvises' shack on the hill.

Day and night there's a light
In my heart that will burn.

She was standing in the open doorway of the shack in a white nightgown, singing to the cold, calm night.

Let the light lead you home
Through the wide open door

She was beautiful, standing there with the light behind her, and her voice was as clear and perfect as a bell.

Straight into my open arms
Forevermore!

Her song echoed across the hills and the sky, and was lost.

28

"Olivia, you and your girls don't stand a chance in this place," Mrs. Clancy said to Mama one day. "This is coal-mining country. A smart woman with two smart girls doesn't belong here. You want your girls to grow up and marry coal miners?"

"But what can I do?" Mama said. "I don't know a soul beyond these hills . . . except a sister in Roanoke."

So they talked about Roanoke, and I could feel a big change coming.

The change taking place inside me was still troublesome, too. Sometimes I felt just like a morning glory opening my face to the sun. But it was a painful kind of awakening. It made my eyes burn, and I would retreat again into the little blue bud. They were strange and bittersweet days, sometimes laced with sorrow too deep for my understanding and sometimes filled with joy too much to bear. I tried to talk to Junie and she tried to understand. But somehow I felt Junie did not come awake like this. Nobody ever felt this way before.

The latest gossip was what in the world Olivia Shortt and her girls were doing hanging around that old witch Clancy all the time for? Mrs. Moore was pea-green. She tried to pick me and Junie about what'd the Clancy house look like on the inside, what'd we talk to that woman about? How come she was so thick with Mama all of a sudden? We just kept our lips sealed and smiled at her. That about infuriated her to death. Funny thing was, nobody latched on to the juiciest piece of gossip, which was turning out to be the truth. Maybe it was because they didn't believe my mama could get a man like Josh Clancy. But Junie and I couldn't help noticing Josh and Mama were falling in love. It made me so mad I couldn't see straight, and Junie thought it was wonderful.

At school the talk about us and Nit had died down. This new development of the Shortts taking up with the Clancys took precedence over any old gossip already talked to death. But I didn't say anything at school either, and after a while the kids stopped asking what was going on.

Then came a joyful day in February when I was at school reading all alone under the old rotten persimmon tree during recess. It was one of those false spring days when the warmth and the smells around you fool you into thinking spring is here. I could hear the little first-graders nearby chanting as they jumped rope. It was the same old chant Junie and I and our friends used to do, and the same chant our grandmothers' grandmothers did back in England and Scotland a hundred years ago.

> *Mother, mother, I feel sick,*
> *Send for the doctor, quick, quick, quick!*

First thing I knew, there was Dora Faye, Susie Ruth, and Hilda Matilda come to sit down beside me on the ground.

"Hidy," they said to me.

"Hidy, strangers," I said. "Long time no see."

"Whatcha reading, Ginny?" Dora Faye said.

"*Anne of Green Gables.*"

"Yeah, I read that," Susie Ruth said. "It's good."

"You don't never come around no more," Tildy said.

"Well . . . I . . ."

No, I couldn't be nasty. They were trying to make up. I just shrugged.

"The club ain't no good without you," Dora Faye went on. "We want you to come back."

Strange thrills ran through me. How I had dreamed they would say this to me!

"Yeah, we want you to come back," Susie Ruth said.

"We tried and tried to write a good play, but nobody can write one like you can."

Did they want me just to write their plays?

"I'll write your plays," I said, nice as I knew how. "I been thinking on a good one . . . but . . . but I don't think I want to be in the club again."

"Why not!" they all said together.

"I don't know. It wouldn't ever be the same again . . . not after what happened."

They looked at me with guilt-stricken faces.

"But I'll write your plays for you, honest I will."

We all fell silent for a moment.

"Just think," Tildy said at last. "We'll be in the seventh grade next fall, and going away to Coaltown to school. We came all this way together. It would be a shame to get away from each other now."

"Sometimes," Dora Faye said solemnly, "sometimes I think about us all growing up together. We had such good times."

"We sure did," Susie Ruth and Tildy agreed.

I couldn't think of a thing to say.

"But you're right, Ginny," Susie Ruth said. "It won't never be the same again."

"We want you, too, Ginny. Not just your plays," from Dora Faye.

Honest to goodness, I thought I'd cry. But I didn't.

"You always had the best ideas, Ginny," Tildy said. "Better than anybody else."

Yes, it was true, I thought. I really did. And it was the first truly good opinion I had had of myself in a long time. A body needs friends, I thought, to make her feel like a body worth noticing.

"Let's play jump rope with those little girls," I said, suddenly feeling childish and giddy.

"Them little first-graders?" Tildy laughed.

"Yeah!" Dora Faye jumped up and grinned. "Just like we used to."

"Come on!"

And for the rest of recess, laughing and squealing and red-faced, we jumped rope with the little young 'uns.

Doctor, doctor, shall I die?
Yes, my child, but do not cry.

29

One Saturday morning when we went to see Mrs. Clancy she was all excited and bright-eyed. "I heard from my sister, Olivia, my sister in Pennsylvania, the one who owns the bookstore I told you about."

"Is that right?"

"She says she needs somebody to help her in the

store. She's willing to give you and your girls room and board for six months till you can get on your feet. And she wants you to work for her."

Just like that? Move to Pennsylvania? Mama sat down quick.

"You have to go soon, or she'll have to get someone else. What do you think, Olivia?"

Mama looked at me and Junie. Junie and I looked at each other. The big change was here.

"I'll be up there in a month with Josh, Olivia. Then we can all help each other. Josh wants you to go."

"Josh wants me to go?" Mama said, like she didn't believe it.

"Of course he does." Mrs. Clancy smiled. "He said be sure and tell you that."

Mama didn't reply, but we knew her mind was racing. Go to Pennsylvania. Work in a bookstore. Be near Josh. Maybe someday marry Josh. Leave this place I have lived in all my life. My girls . . .

"I just kept thinking and thinking," Mrs. Clancy went on. "And I thought I don't want to lose you, or your girls. So I wrote to my sister about you. And she's willing to help. She's a good person."

"What do you think, girls?" Mama said at last.

"Whatever you say, Mama," I said, holding my breath.

"What about the fare up there? I don't have a cent to my name."

"Josh will give it to you," Mrs. Clancy said.

"Well . . . my old furniture isn't worth moving," Mama said slowly. "But what about my house?"

"Let Poppy take care of that!" Junie said. "Let him sell it and send you your share of the money."

"All right!" Mama said, and clapped her hands together like a little girl.

Then we were all shouting and jumping up and down in the middle of the rose room. It was like we had just won a big prize.

So we talked about Pennsylvania, all of us talking at once. Mrs. Clancy told us everything she could remember about the people, the climate, the schools . . .

Then suddenly there came a scream from outside— no, not just a scream, a death cry. It chilled me so I couldn't move. Mama, Junie, and Mrs. Clancy went rushing past me out to the front of the house, slamming the door behind them. I sat like a stone. I knew what was wrong.

I finally moved toward the door like slow motion in the movies. It was like I had gone through all this before. I knew each second what was going to happen next. There was me touching and turning the glass doorknob; it sparkled in my hand. And outside there was the cold sun shining white on my face; and there was Nit Purvis running downhill after something or somebody; and there was Mama and Mrs. Clancy and

Junie running, too; and there was this thing they were all running after—on fire—also running; and there was me suddenly with my own screams blending with Lou Jean's because I knew she had done it at last. The screams still go on, forever echoing and reechoing through the rugged hills of Virginia.

O lost, and by the wind grieved, ghost, come back again!

30

I remember every detail of Lou Jean's funeral. I remember how the people were packed in the white church, arm to arm. I can still smell the flowers, and that smell still makes me sick. I remember how it rained when her body was taken to the graveyard on the hill to be buried. I remember all the black umbrellas loaned by the funeral director. I watched the water bead up on her casket and roll off onto the imitation grass below. I watched the water making little rivers around my worn-out shoes, and Nit standing there in the downpour crying his heart out while somebody held an umbrella over him. I watched Mrs. Purvis's face, broken into a million pieces. Her hair had turned white as the snow that had all melted away. Now there was only the rain.

"We are special, Ginny," I could hear Lou Jean saying on the long-ago brilliant summer day. "You and me and Junie will live forever."

And the rain continued to pour down. It seemed the sky was grieving with us on this sorry day when we had to bury our Lou Jean. And it seemed like the sun would never shine again. Everybody we knew in the world was there, even Poppy, even the Clancys. The Jenkinses were there, the Looneys, the Ratliffs, the Esteps, and Mrs. Moore with her bunch of redheaded kids.

But I didn't care. I didn't care about any of these people anymore. They killed her, and it was too late to show her their respect. I wouldn't talk to any of them ever again. I just wanted to go away to Pennsylvania and be rid of them.

After the funeral, Poppy said goodbye quickly and was gone. I didn't even kiss him goodbye. I just turned away with Mama, Junie, and the Clancys. We went to the Clancys' for tea. I curled up on one end of the rose couch and watched the rain out the window running off the roof of the house. Junie sat on the other end of the couch, all wrapped up in her own thoughts.

Josh sat down between me and Junie, but I didn't look at him. He grunted and lit a cigarette.

"You know," he said to me after a while. "I really

didn't mean to kill your dog. It was a dreadful accident, and I'm sorry. You must learn to forgive."

I went on watching the rain. I remembered the day Josh saved Lou Jean from falling into the slate dump.

Josh pointed to the portrait over the fireplace. "Those were my sisters who died," he said. "The little one, Shirley, was much like you."

I looked straight at him then.

"She had a dog, too, and she was afraid of horses. She loved this room. She loved the ticking of the clocks."

"Really and truly?"

"Really and truly." Josh smiled at me and for the first time I grudgingly admitted he wasn't half bad to look at.

"Why do you have so many clocks?" Junie asked.

"It was Dad's collection. He collected clocks—all shapes and sizes—as you can see, for years. And he made the shelves for Shirley so she could hear them all ticking at the same time and place. Dad and Shirley used to come in here and sit together, just listening to the clocks tick."

Tears came to my eyes again. "M-maybe that's why her t-time ran out so soon," I stammered. "All these clocks were eating up her time."

Josh and Junie both laughed a little.

"No, no," Josh said, and patted my head. "That's not possible, Ginny. Time moves only at a certain pace, no matter how many clocks you have."

I knew that! Of course I knew that! I wasn't stupid! But I had to find some reason for a little girl to die . . . For Lou Jean, too. Didn't there have to be a reason?

Tears were pouring down my face again. "It's not fair!" I said between clenched teeth. "It's just not fair!"

"It is my personal belief, Ginny"—Josh tried to console me—"that life is always fair. It just doesn't seem fair when you see only part of the picture. But in the end, I believe the scales always balance out."

"But why must they go away?" I said. "They'll all go away from me someday."

"People do die," he said. "It's one of those facts of life. But if you really love someone, Ginny, they always come back to you . . . Maybe in another form, but they come back. Your love will draw them back."

They always come back to you in another form! It was the truth I already knew, but was afraid to put into words. It was just what I needed to hear.

"Oh, Josh, do you really mean it?" I said.

"Do you really believe it?" Junie said, and I knew she had been thinking along the same lines.

"With all my heart," Josh said.

In that instant, I forgave Josh Clancy everything.

"Do you think we will meet Lou Jean again?"

"I have no doubt of it, Ginny."

A long silence followed while we all looked at each other thoughtfully.

Later Junie and I were sitting in the Clancy kitchen peeling potatoes when I looked up all of a sudden and there were the ghost girls standing in the kitchen doorway looking at us.

"Junie."

"What is it?"

Her eyes followed mine.

"Do you see them, Junie?"

"Yeah, I see them. It's the first time we have both seen them at the same time."

The vision faded, and we never saw them again.

That night the rain turned to sleet, and as I looked at the cold mountaintops, I remembered watching for Santa Claus to come leaping over those mountains in his sleigh when I was such a little girl on Christmas Eve. I knew I would never believe in Santa Claus again, or in witches, but I had something so much better to believe in.

I would never jump rope or play like or cut out paper dolls again. Never would I go into those hills again—not to ramble in the golden leaves, or to sing to the trees from my cliff stage, or to scamper up a tower that touched the clouds, or to swing on a vine. Never again would I fly on the magic wings of childhood—at least, not in this life.

31

The next day we left Sweet Creek Holler—Mama, Junie, and I. Josh took us to Bluefield, West Virginia, where we caught a train for Pennsylvania.

When Josh said goodbye to Mama, he kissed her full on the lips and she kissed him back. Junie and I grinned at each other.

Then he turned to me and Junie and kissed us each on the cheek. "I'll see you girls in about a month," he said. "You be good and take care of your mother."

"We will," we said.

Then he hugged Mama again and left. She wiped a tear off her cheek and hustled us aboard the train. That evening, for the first time, I could see firsthand that two things I had learned in school were absolutely true: One, that many folks in the world don't have fair skin, blond hair, and blue eyes; and, two, that the world is a ball instead of a hole.

Yes, I thought, there is a whole 'nother world out there, and I would see it.

Late in the night, I looked out at the strange, flat land, and I could hear a train whistle blowing. The amazing thing was I was on that train. I thought of old Buddy and Daddy, my friends and teachers, Poppy, and, most of all, Lou Jean. Then I slept and dreamed I could hear Sweet Creek rippling over the rocks outside my bedroom window. And in her ripple I heard the long-ago, the lost, the far echo of laughter—the laughter of little girls running in the sunshine of another time, unafraid.